The Last Stand

Editor: Talia Leduc


ISBN-13: 978-1990590498

Give feedback on the book at:
lorhainneeckhart@hotmail.com

Twitter: @LEckhart
Facebook: AuthorLorhainneEckhart

Printed in the U.S.A

# THE LAST STAND

## Billy Jo McCabe Mystery

## LORHAINNE ECKHART

---

## Billy Jo McCabe Mystery

---

Nothing As It Seems
Hiding in Plain Sight
The Cold Case
The Trap
Above the Law
The Stranger at the Door
The Children
The Last Stand
The Charity

The social worker and the cop, an unlikely couple drawn together on a small, secluded Pacific Northwest island where nothing is as it seems. Protecting the innocent comes at a cost, and what seems to be a sleepy, quiet town is anything but.

**The Social Worker**

Billy Jo McCabe wants only to help children overcome their troubled lives, as she herself struggles to forget the childhood nightmare she survived. She took sociology and prelaw at the insistence of her adoptive father, Chase McCabe, and learned how to use power tools from her adoptive mother, Rose. She loves reading in the backs of bookstores before tucking the book back on the shelf and slipping out without paying. She has a fondness for peanut butter and dill pickle sandwiches, has a three-legged cat named Harley, hates running (because that was all she did as a kid), and secretly binges on brownies and red wine on the sofa in front of her TV every Friday night.

She's never been married and has dated only twice. She visits Chase and Rose when summoned and shows up dutifully for every holiday with her family, but she has no siblings to speak of, and she feels a growing resentment for the mother who abandoned her in foster care. Despite proudly maintaining the same prickly attitude that nearly landed her behind bars as a kid, she has yet to speak up to Chase, who interferes in her life too frequently, ready to fix every problem, whether she wants him to or not.

One thing no one knows about Billy Jo is that she moved to Roche Harbor because it's the only clue she has about the last known whereabouts of the woman who abandoned her.

**The Cop**

Mark Friessen, son of Jed and Diana Friessen, has landed accidently in the role of small-town detective, a position in which he's going nowhere. Nearly married once, and broken-hearted three times, he's sworn he'll stay single forever, and he keeps his tattoo of a former girlfriend as a reminder that only fools fall in love. He's tall, attractive, and stubborn, and he refuses to live in the shadow of his two older brothers, Chris and Danny.

As Roche Harbor's youngest detective, he sleeps with a gun under his pillow. He has a stray dog that won't leave, and he swears that the only two food groups that exist are meat and potatoes. His favorite drink is black coffee in the morning, sugared coffee in the afternoon, and a shot of whiskey in his coffee at night to keep him warm.

*****Each book in this series is a complete book, with no cliff-hangers, and can be read as a standalone. However, these books may contain references to situations from earlier books in the series. As with any long book series that focuses on specific characters, their changing relationships, and how their lives continue to unfold, you may find it more enjoyable to read the series in order of publishing, as there will be developments and changes in the relationship dynamics of the core characters.*

**The law is the law until someone comes after your family.**

**From *New York Times* & *USA Today* bestselling author Lorhainne Eckhart comes a new Billy Jo McCabe mystery set on a small island town in the Pacific Northwest. On the eve of Police Chief Mark Friessen's wedding, a fierce snowstorm blankets the island, knocking out power, and the body of a woman is discovered in the church. The only clue is the note in her hand, a list of names—all members of Mark's family.**

Mark Friessen has been counting down the days to his wedding to Billy Jo McCabe. Yet only days from Christmas, after their families arrive, a freak blizzard comes out of nowhere and knocks out power on the entire island.

With the island in an emergency and the ferry shut down, no help is arriving anytime soon from the mainland. Mark receives a call to stop into the church where he and Billy Jo are planning on being married the next day, but there he stumbles upon the body of a woman. The only evidence is a note she's clutching. At the top, in all bold, is the word *KILL*, and listed below are the names of everyone he loves, including Billy Jo, his parents, his brothers, their wives, and his two nieces.

With access to the outside world cut off, Mark finds himself up against an invisible enemy who he believes is coming after his unsuspecting family. But Mark has no idea who it is. Where is the killer hiding on the island, why isn't Mark's name on the list, and who is the dead woman? Mark is determined to find the killer and protect his family, whatever it takes…even if it's his *Last Stand*.

"*This is a story I personally don't want to believe is possible, but in today's world it is, unfortunately, too believable, and horrifying.*"

Catlou

"*It's a deeply emotional story that is all too real. Lorhainne Eckhart once again brings strong characters in Billy Jo and Mark and takes them on a suspenseful and heartbreaking ride and had me glued to the pages reading.*"

Bleem58, Bookbub

"This story is twisty, shocking and even nearly unbearable at moments, but above all it is absolutely unputdownable. Readers will discover the tenacious strength of will, the resolve and courage of not only Mark and Billy Jo, but their families as well."

Rebmay

## Chapter 1

Mark stared at the weekly report of problems, a revolving door of the same people, those he could do something about and those who just got better at hiding their crimes. He heard the knock on his door just as he took a swallow of coffee, and he turned where he was standing beside his desk.

"Hey, Chief," said Carmen. "Just got a call from Lisa Jenkins about a man who's openly threatening her. His hostility is over the top, so much so that she fears for her safety. She said she showed up for a wellness check on his kids and believes he's hurting them and interfering with her taking them."

He just stared at Carmen as she shrugged on her heavy coat, wondering whether he was supposed to know who Lisa Jenkins was. Maybe his expression gave him away. He set down the printed three-page report, which had been waiting on his desk when he walked in an hour earlier.

"Taking kids, wellness checks? You lost me. Who is this?" He let out a heavy sigh, feeling the weight of everything. His parents were on their way, his brothers, their families, and Billy-Jo's family. He still needed to pay the restaurant, pick up his new suit, and make sure he stopped in at the church at some point that day to make sure everything was a go for the wedding. He gave his head a shake, willing himself to get back in the game.

"Lisa…" Carmen said. "You know, the junior social worker brought in to help with the rise in the case load? For your fiancée."

Right. He thought Billy Jo had mentioned that at the church before their meeting with the minister who would listen as they said "I do" and officially pronounce them mister and missus. Maybe that was why he was feeling a gigantic pressure right in the middle of his chest. Mark reached for his cell phone on his desk but saw no message from Billy Jo.

"Billy Jo didn't call," he said. "Is she there too?" He had his phone to his ear already, and it was ringing, but it went right to voicemail.

"Hello, this is Billy Jo McCabe, with DCFS. I can't take your call right now. Leave me a message and I'll call you back when I can. If this is an emergency…"

He hung up. Right, she wasn't going in to work that day because Chase and Rose were flying in, and she was doing all the last-minute stuff involving her dress and something else he couldn't remember.

He realized Carmen was still standing there. "No answer." He held his phone up. "I'll come with you. Have you met this Lisa?" He reached for his keys in his drawer and shoved his phone in his pocket, looking to Carmen as he strode over to the coat tree and reached for his black down winter coat. His gun was holstered on his favorite blue jeans, and his sheriff's badge was pinned to his shirt.

"Only once," she said. "She's young. Don't think she's been doing this long. You want to follow me?"

Mark shrugged on his coat. "Yeah. So tell me again who she is and what's going on. Would have thought this would go through Billy Jo. You said this social worker is taking the kids? She's supposed to call us first, or have I missed something?"

Carmen had already pulled open the door to the station and was walking out. A blast of cold swept over him as he glanced back to his dog's empty bed. Billy Jo had Lucky at home. Maybe that was also why he felt so off that day. His routine was being completely screwed up.

"Lacy," he called out.

"I already know," the dispatcher replied. "I took the call and patched it through to Carmen." She was behind her desk, Gail's old desk, and she gestured to him as she stood up. So damn efficient, but he wondered when he'd stop comparing her to Gail. "You'll be at the Clarks'. I got it." She just lifted her hand, and Mark took in Elisha's empty desk, as well, knowing she was already doing rounds on the island.

"Well, good," he said. "If Billy Jo calls, tell her to call me."

He didn't miss what he thought was the hint of a smile tugging at the older woman's lips. Her hair was a mix of dark and white, and he was pretty sure she was as tall as Gail.

He stepped out of the office and kept walking down the steps, feeling the icy chill. The salt on the steps crunched under his cowboy boots. Heavy clouds loomed overhead, but he knew it was too cold for rain.

Carmen was already in the sheriff's cruiser as Mark pulled open the door of his Jeep and started the engine. Carmen backed out, swinging around and flicking on her siren. So they were there, kids in trouble, a desperate situation. Damn, he hated that. He wished Billy Jo had filled him in more on this Lisa.

He followed Carmen as she pulled down a road he was familiar with and took in the houses so close together. Cars pulled over to the side as they flew past another road, more trees and privacy. Carmen pulled up in front of a small older two-story. He could see a man in the doorway, dark skinned, tall, lanky, and a woman on the porch.

Carmen was parked behind a burgundy Hyundai, and Mark stopped in front, turning off his engine, feeling his sidearm. He stepped out of the Jeep, his coat now zipped, and reached for his brown knit hat in his pocket. As he pulled it on, feeling the bite of cold, he strode across the grass, Carmen already two steps ahead of him.

"Thank goodness you're here," the young woman said. "This man is preventing me from doing my job. He's openly harassed me and been verbally abusive…"

"I did no such thing, you lying bitch. You showed up here, coming in my house, disrespecting me," the man cut in. He wore a long-sleeved faded brown shirt and what looked like sweatpants. He had no coat. Mark figured the woman was Lisa, who had called.

"Okay, so what exactly is going on here?" Mark said, resting his foot on the bottom step.

Lisa was young, early twenties, he thought, wearing

dark-rimmed glasses and holding a clipboard close to her chest. He glanced once to Carmen, who appeared right beside him. Mark was very aware of the man's anger toward Lisa. He stepped up onto the porch, looking down on her, putting himself between them.

"And you are?" he said to the man.

"That's Nathan Clark," Lisa cut in behind him, and he didn't miss the snark in her tone. He glanced back once to her, knowing Nathan was fisting his hands. Just her opening her mouth had provoked him.

He turned back to Nathan, who looked past him with dark eyes locked on to the short social worker. He knew when a man had been pushed too far. "Nathan, I'm Chief Friessen. We got a call about some trouble…"

The man was already shaking his head and had pulled his arms across his chest. He had to be cold. Mark took in the closed screen door and could hear voices inside, a woman and kids, he thought.

"Look, I don't know what she's yapping on about, but she showed up here, walking through my house, and yelled at me to get away from her when I did nothing. She was the one disrespecting me and my wife. She's going on about us hurting our kids, which is an outright lie…"

"I'm just doing my job," Lisa said. "You have no right to interfere, and that was exactly what you were doing in there, following me right on my heels and yelling at me, scaring me. This is a state matter, and you are interfering—"

"These are my kids," Nathan said. "You coming in here, turning your nose up at me and—"

"Hey, hey, enough," Mark said. "Just cool down, both of you. Nathan, give us a minute." He turned to the new social worker and wondered why Billy Jo hadn't called him. "Come with me. I want to talk to you."

He went down the steps, seeing her legs were bare under her coat. She wore a short dress underneath, he thought, and light brown ankle boots. He gestured to her and then took in Carmen, who said nothing as she stood there. He had only to nod before he heard her say something to the father, who was standing guard at that door.

He turned around, taking in how short Lisa was, about Billy Jo's height. She really looked like a kid. "What's going on here? Billy Jo sent you?" They were far enough away that he couldn't hear what the father was saying to Carmen, but he could see how upset he was.

"I'm the social worker on call today, and this is a wellness check. A complaint came in, and it was given to me. This has nothing to do with Billy Jo, who's away now. Everything will come through me until she's back from her time off."

The way she was looking at him, he realized she didn't have a clue who she was, but then, he knew Billy Jo didn't go around sharing her personal business. Evidently, Lisa wasn't in the know.

"Billy Jo is getting married to me. I'm her fiancé. You should know, filling in for her, that we have a protocol on the island. In any cases where you're removing a child, you are required to contact my office, and a deputy is to accompany you." He kept his voice low.

When she looked up at him, he could see she wasn't on the same page, maybe because she was shaking her head. "With all due respect, Chief, this was not a visit where I planned to take the kids. But, just showing up here and seeing what I saw, I'm alarmed. The condition of the premises, the dirt, the locked doors…and there was feces on the floor. The father is volatile, and the kids appear unbathed. One little girl, who I understand has special needs, appears neglected." She was so damn matter of fact, and he sensed she would argue about everything.

"Volatile? I think you need to be a little more specific about what your concerns are. You suspect abuse, hurting his kids?" He gestured, wondering why she had a clipboard.

"You saw him up there, the way he looked at me, yelling at me. He stalked behind me in the house when I expected answers from him. He was disrespectful…"

Mark angled his head. He wanted to call Billy Jo again, but if he did, he knew her well enough to know she'd likely be in her car and on her way over there. Maybe there was something more about this situation that he didn't know.

"You showed up here about his kids. I'm seeing a father who's trying to protect them. You want to take his kids away? I would be surprised if a father let you do that without fighting back. You want to walk me inside and show me what the issues are?"

The way she pulled the clipboard up close to her chest, he wondered if she'd say no. "Fine, but I'll need your assistance getting the kids out of the house. This is a state decision, and I'm acting on behalf of the state. I'll need to take the kids, all of them, to the hospital for a doctor to look them over."

Then she turned and started walking back to the

house, and Mark followed, seeing that Carmen and Nathan were staring at him long and hard.

"I'm going in the house with Lisa," he said. "Nathan, Carmen will stay outside with you. We won't be a minute."

Lisa had pulled open the screen and walked right in, and Mark reached for the door.

Nathan lifted his hands in the air and linked them behind his head in frustration. "Fine. My wife is there."

"How many kids?" he asked. He could hear Lisa inside, speaking with the kind of voice that expected answers, but about what, he didn't know.

"Two girls, two and five," Nathan said.

He only nodded and walked inside, taking in the small entry, the wood floors, an older sectional with piles of clothes on it, a laundry basket, toys and papers scattered on the floor. A woman with dark hair, a few inches taller than Lisa, was holding a towel. Her hair was half out of a ponytail.

"Down here, Chief," Lisa said to him as she gestured to a narrow hall with doors closed. He only nodded at the woman standing there, wide-eyed, a little girl jumping around her with a thumb in her mouth. Then he realized another girl was there, naked, her hair a mess, shoving ripped paper into her mouth.

"No, no, no, Mellie," the woman said and ran over to the little girl to pull the paper from her mouth. The girl squealed and swatted at her.

Mark saw the mother struggling, and he took in something smeared on the wall in the hall. He could smell it from there and knew it was feces. The social worker was looking at him expectantly as she stood by a door locked with a deadbolt, which needed a key, and another door with a sliding bolt.

"Every door here, all four, has a lock on it," Lisa said. "Do they lock the kids in? I'm sure you can smell that a child defecated, and it's on the walls. One has no clothes on, and there's something wrong with the other, too. The place is a mess. The kitchen is not the neatest I've seen, and there's food in the corner on the floor."

He slid the bolt on one of the doors and opened it to see a bathroom—not a mess but reasonable, with a towel on a hook, toothbrushes by the sink, and a bathtub with no shower curtain.

"Look, I don't know what to say," Mark said. "I see the mess. Is there something wrong with the one screaming out there?" He glanced down the hall. Everything in the house felt tense, but then, he supposed having DCFS show up like this only ramped up family problems.

"Special needs, I think. Not really sure, but something is wrong…" She was flipping through her chart, lifting papers and reading, and then she shook her head and let out an exasperated breath. "But, regardless, the care is seriously lacking. I'll need some help getting the kids loaded up. I think I've seen enough here." She clutched her clipboard to her chest. The way she said it had been dismissive, and damn, did he hate this. She brushed past him, leaving him standing there.

"Okay, I'm taking the kids," she said. "Are there car seats? I need clothes on these girls, too…"

She was cold, unfeeling. Nothing about this felt right. The mother wore a look he knew too well, shell-shock. He put his hand on the screen door and pushed it open, and Nathan and Carmen both stopped talking and looked at him.

"Your kids in there," he said. "Something wrong with the little girl with no clothes on?"

The man was much calmer now. He wondered what Carmen had said to him. "My older one, she's five. One doctor said she's got autism, another said rett syndrome. Can't keep no clothes on her. She takes them off as soon as they're on."

Mark realized Carmen hadn't looked away from Nathan, yet she said nothing. "You have locks on the doors in there. You lock the kids in?"

Nathan shook his head and gestured. "No, sir, no way. Those locks are to keep Mellie out. She wears a diaper, but we can't keep it on her. We lock the doors because she goes in and wipes her shit on the walls everywhere, so we have to keep her in one small part of the house. Look, we're doing the best we can, but I'm not always here. I have to work off island a lot, and it's just my wife here. My daughter, she screams if you try to brush her hair. Can't get socks on her at all. I tried to explain all that to the social worker in there, but she wouldn't hear none of it…"

"Hey, Nathan, I get it," Carmen cut in. "You just need some help, is all. Sometimes these state workers only check boxes and can't see or hear anything. I know you're just trying to protect your family, and I can hear how upset you are. She probably didn't understand all that. She's not from around here and doesn't know you."

Damn, how did Carmen do that? The door squeaked open behind them.

"Chief Friessen, I'm ready to go," Lisa said. "Can you get some car seats so I can take the kids?" There was something so inexperienced about the social worker. She had so much to learn about people.

"I have car seats, but I want the name of your supervisor," Nathan said.

Lisa was still standing in the doorway. "My direct supervisor is away right now. You want the name of my acting supervisor this week?" Now she sounded way too helpful.

"I do, name and phone number. I'm calling and making a formal complaint about you."

He wondered whether Lisa would say no, but she only shrugged and said, "Sure. Grant—"

"Billy Jo is in charge here. Pretty sure you report to her," Mark couldn't help himself from saying.

Lisa seemed to stiffen and then shook her head. "Ms. McCabe is away, and that's not how the chain of command works. Grant is who I report to right now." Damn, she was so matter of fact. "You have a pen?"

Carmen, bless her, pulled one from her pocket along with paper and handed it to Nathan, who was going to have his kids pulled out of there. Mark listened to her rattle off Grant's name and number.

"I'll help you with the car seats," Mark said to Nathan. He listened to screaming in the house as he followed him down the stairs and over to an older off-white minivan, and all he could think was that nothing about this seemed right.

---

## Chapter 2

---

"I don't know what's keeping Mark," Billy Jo said. "I know he should be here by now. Damn, it's really coming down out there..." She fumbled her glass of wine then, spilling some of the red she loved on the light granite island. Her mom and Diana were sitting at high-back chairs across from her, each with a glass of wine, and she could hear the voices of her dad and Mark's dad, Jed, in the living room.

"I'll get that," said her mom, already off her chair, her long blond hair hanging loose past her shoulders. She wore a pink turtleneck and deep blue wool pants, but she could wear anything and look good. She reached for a sponge at the sink and moved Billy Jo over as she wiped up the spill and handed her the glass. "Here you go. You just drink your wine before you knock something else over. Why don't you sit down and let us know what else we still have to do?"

Diana smiled at her. "You indulged us for the day, letting us drag you around town, so let us wait on you now."

Billy Jo took a swallow of her wine. Through the big windows, a heavy snow was starting to settle in the darkness. She pulled at the hem of her black cardigan over a pair of black dressy slacks and a sleeveless silky black shirt. The only things not black were the fluffy brown slippers on her feet. She had to remind herself she looked good, chasing away the voice of doubt that at one time had taken up too many hours, lingering in her head. The wedding had seemed so far away, but she was now staring down the moment she and Mark would stand before the minister and say "I do." Good God, maybe that was why she was so freaked out.

"You want to call Mark?" Diana said, leaning an elbow on the island. "What time are we meeting up at the restaurant? Danny, J.D., Chris, Evie, and the girls should be here and checked into the hotel by now. I don't know how you do it with the ferries, having to wait to get on and off island. Although it's beautiful here, I never realized how cut off you are." She wore a deep green knit sweater that made her vivid blue eyes pop. At least now Billy Jo knew where Mark got his blue eyes and red hair from. There was nothing about Diana that she disliked. "You know, when Mark first told me about you, Billy Jo, I told Jed I thought he'd met the one."

She didn't know what to say. She took in Mark's mom, who was so warm and welcoming, and she wondered how much Mark had shared about her. Did Diana really understand who Billy Jo was?

"I recognize that look," Diana said. "You have the pre-wedding jitters."

Billy Jo pulled her arm over the flat of her stomach as she held her wine, not looking over to her mom, who she knew likely wanted to add something. "I'm not nervous. Why, do I look nervous?" Even she could hear how defensive she sounded. She took in the diamond ring on her finger, which she hadn't taken off since Mark put it on. When she lifted her gaze, her mom rose a brow and dumped the sponge back in the sink.

"If you're not, I'd think there was something wrong," Diana said. "You're right, it really is coming down out there. Jed, what time was the reservation tonight?"

She could see her dad and Jed from where she stood. Jed was lounging on the new blue sectional, her dad in the easy chair.

"Six," he said. "Aren't we still waiting on Mark? What time is it, anyway?"

Something about Jed Friessen was so much like his son. Billy Jo was vaguely listening to the back and forth when she felt the touch on her arm, her mom. She took in the clock on the stove, seeing it was nearly five.

"You okay?" Rose said. "You've been unusually quiet today, letting us drag you around into shops I know you have no interest in. I know how uncomfortable you get, being the center of attention."

Her shoulders were tight, and she made herself take another sip of wine. Just then, she heard the door, and she let out a heavy sigh. "Just out of my comfort zone…" she started.

In the living room, Mark said something to Lucky, who trotted to the door and took in her cat, Harley, who was curled up fast asleep on the cat tree next to the window.

"Hey, everyone. Sorry I'm late," Mark said. "It's

really coming down out there. Billy Jo, the shed door was wide open."

She shrugged. "Wasn't me," she said, gesturing, and he gave her one of those heavy gazes.

"You sure?"

She really looked at him.

"Maybe it was the wind," he said. "I can't remember ever seeing the snow coming down the way it is. Reminds me of home, not the island. The roads aren't pretty out there."

She didn't move from where she stood, holding her wine, taking in Mark, who was brushing the snow from his hair. He was sock-footed as he walked right over to her, his heavy coat still on, and leaned down and pressed a kiss to her lips. For a second, it was just the two of them, and she wondered whether he was going to start in about the shed again, but when he pulled back, he let his complicated gaze linger, and she looked up into it.

"I called you and you didn't answer," he said. "Sent you a text, too. Kind of started off the morning with an issue."

Her brow furrowed. Mark pulled open the fridge behind her and reached for a beer, then twisted off the cap and smiled to his mom, but Billy Jo just stared up at him, keeping her back to everyone.

"You talk to your brothers?" Diana said to him. Jed was now standing behind his wife, his hands resting on her shoulders. Billy Jo looked over, a knot in her stomach over the issue Mark had mentioned.

"No, been a crazy day," he said. "Was going to stop in at the hotel. I think they were coming in on the three o'clock ferry…" He scratched his head and took a swallow of his beer, still standing right in her space.

"I'll call Danny, see where they are." Jed had his phone out already and was dialing, and he turned away, taking a few steps.

Billy Jo rested her glass of wine on the counter. When Mark went to step away, she reached for his arm and pulled him back. "My phone is turned off in the bottom of my purse. Pretty sure you're the one who told me that taking time off meant turning my phone off and keeping it off. You have no idea how difficult it was for me not to check it every twenty seconds. But, again, didn't you say to me this morning before leaving that I should enjoy the day with our moms and not take calls from work?"

He made a face. "Didn't think you'd listen, and I kind of didn't mean calls from me."

She angled her head, wondering how he expected her to just pick and choose which calls to answer. Her parents and Diana were talking in the background, and she glanced back to them, knowing she was supposed to be focused one hundred percent on the wedding.

"What happened?" she said, staring up at Mark, and even she could hear the edge in her voice. She knew so well the many moods of Mark, and the grim edge he had in his expression made the knot tighten in her stomach. She wanted to groan.

"Got a call at the station from that new junior social worker, Lisa…?"

"Jenkins," she cut in. Tension now pulled right across her shoulders. Maybe Mark knew she was one step from getting on her phone and calling the office to find out everything, as he put his beer on the island and slid his hand over her shoulder. "What happened?"

He shook his head. "She was at a house, making a

call on a family, and called the station with a complaint that she was being threatened. It was Nathan Clark, with two little girls. I can tell by your face that you know who I'm talking about. But she hadn't called the station for anyone to go with her. Does she not get the protocol here?"

She stared at Mark and blinked, then opened her mouth to say something, but instead she wanted to pick up the phone and call Lisa, the new girl Grant had sent over. Just what the hell did she think she was doing?

"Seriously?" she said. "I have half a mind to call her, then Pam, then Grant. I went over everything with her, and she basically cut me off, saying she knew her job and she understood. Told me to enjoy my time off, and congrats on the wedding, and not to worry about anything. Now I'm freaking out. Why was she at the Clarks'? Did something happen? I know Nathan and his wife, Grace. They have two girls and really struggle. The oldest has Rett syndrome, and I'm pretty sure the other has something wrong, too. Those two parents are really doing the best they can. I know Nathan was working two jobs to pay their bills. Do you know how long it took him to get a doctor to actually diagnose his kid? And I know what it cost him: a lot of money they didn't have."

She pressed her hands to her face and pulled them away, realizing how quiet it was. Her mom and dad and Jed and Diana were watching them. Judging by their faces, they had heard.

"Please tell me you handled it," she continued. "Damn, I should call Grace and Nathan, make sure they know they have my support… Wait, why did she show up there to begin with?" Everyone was watching her as she narrowed her gaze, looking up to Mark.

He shook his head. "Not much I could do except become a buffer. The house was a mess, with locks on the doors. Lisa had made her mind up and was taking the kids. Social services has jurisdiction, you know that. I did fill Lisa in on her responsibility to call the station first, but not sure she agreed. I have no idea who sent her. She said it was a wellness check or something. They're struggling. Maybe they'll get some help. I know she took the kids to the hospital, strapped them both in the back of her little car. One was screaming. Told Nathan he needed some help…"

She groaned, and maybe that was why Mark had stopped talking. "Helping them doesn't mean yanking their kids," she said. "You're right that they have no help, no support, because it costs money they don't have. The pitiful resources available are allocated based on a waitlist, where they're behind hundreds of other families. Their eldest is still in a diaper, which I'm aware she won't keep on. She's unresponsive, doesn't talk. Grace has no help, but those kids are not abused." She made herself stop talking.

"Is there something I can do, sweetheart?" Chase said from where he stood behind her mom. She knew he meant well, but she shook her head and lifted her hands helplessly.

"No. Thanks, though. If Lisa did what I think she did—no, sorry, what I know she did, those girls are now stuffed in someone's house, an emergency placement. The real kicker is that those kids are now with someone who has no clue what to do or how to handle a child as unresponsive as their eldest, so she'll be locked in a room or tied down, but that isn't considered abuse when it's not done by her parents."

No one said anything. The joy and happiness that had filled the house moments earlier had completely vanished.

---

## Chapter 3

---

The table reserved at the hotel, set for twelve, overlooked the harbor through big windows. The snow had turned into full whiteout conditions, so the drive over had been challenging. Mark sat at the end with his brothers, Danny and Chris. Both had short red hair, but Chris also had a short beard and mustache. Damn, he had missed his brothers.

"Man, I never thought we'd see the day you'd be domesticated," Danny teased.

Mark glanced down the table to his parents and his sisters-in-law, J.D. and Evie, as well as his two nieces, who had each grown a foot. Billy Jo's chair beside him was empty.

"Everything okay with your bride-to-be?" Danny continued. "She's pretty quiet."

Mark glanced over his shoulder from the private alcove where they were dining. He could just make out Billy Jo by the front door of the restaurant, the phone to her ear. He turned back to his brothers, but his mom slid back her chair and walked across the restaurant to Billy Jo.

"Afraid I dumped something on her just as we were leaving," he said. "Someone who's filling in for her did something she's trying to undo."

His brothers exchanged a glance, and he knew he sounded cryptic. He was kicking himself, because now Billy Jo was completely focused on two kids he couldn't do a damn thing about. Mark didn't like feeling helpless. He felt responsible even though it didn't make a lick of sense. His brothers lifted their gazes just as Billy Jo reappeared and sat down beside him.

"So, anything?" he said.

She reached for her glass of water and took a long swallow before shaking her head and looking over to him, shrugging. His heart sank. The happiness that had filled her eyes just that morning had been replaced by a sadness he hadn't seen in a long time.

"I called and spoke with Nathan, who was beside himself. Said he called Grant to lodge a complaint about Lisa. He told me she stared him down as if he were something vile, and she had her mind made up the minute he opened the door. She barged in and wouldn't take no for an answer, tossing out insults and accusations, and it didn't matter what he said.

"He was furious and wanted to know why she was on his doorstep to begin with, which is exactly what I wanted to know. He's been trying to find out where the girls are. I called Lisa twice, and it went right to voicemail. Pretty sure she's screening her calls. I had already left a message for Grant, but he likely isn't going to call me back, so I called Pam at home and found out what I needed.

"It seems the minute I left the office yesterday, little Miss Jenkins was in my office, going through files. She asked Pam to pull up every case, anything that was flagged, and apparently she's taken it upon herself to start doing impromptu no-notice wellness checks—you know, just showing up on a doorstep to catch families off guard. She's pulled three other kids from their homes and placed them in foster care, two off island.

"I found out that the hospital ordered psychiatric care for Nathan and Grace's eldest girl, and the youngest is with another family I hadn't finished vetting. There's nothing I can do about it, because Lisa sounded the alarm and has the state authority behind her. Undoing what she did will take a long time. The kids will be separated, and with the courts closing down for the holidays, they'll be left with strangers." She let out a heavy sigh. "Sorry to put a damper on the night," she said to his brothers before reaching for her red wine and taking a swallow.

"Don't apologize for wanting to help some kids," Chris said. "That's shitty, what happened. So there's nothing you can do?"

Danny, a lawyer, was looking down and shaking his head. "Happens too often. Some social worker sounds an alarm and a family's lives are ripped apart. The system doesn't exactly work in favor of the ones scraping by. Do what you can, Billy Jo, but you also can't stop living."

Mark really looked at his brother, because that was something he'd never heard him say before. "Sounds like there's a story there," he said, resting his arm over the back of Billy Jo's chair, letting his hand linger on her shoulder. Damn, he couldn't believe there was only one more day before they were official. Billy Jo looked up at him, and for a moment he wondered if she'd pull into herself.

Danny lifted his glass of the local amber on tap. "Isn't there always? Yeah, it'll eat you up if you let it, and then you're no use to anyone." He took a big swallow of his beer, looking over to him and then Billy Jo, who was leaning closer to him. "There are days I tell Evie I want out. I wish I had Dad's love of horses and the land, but no, I have to follow in Mom's footsteps, because I want to help people who are chewed up by the law. I don't know. It seems the more I navigate a system that should protect the people it doesn't, the more I see how rigged it is…"

Danny leaned back and lifted his hand, and Mark realized how out of touch he was with his family. "But we're not here to talk about everything that's wrong with the world. We're here in the middle of nowhere, on an island, to get you married off. Hey, everyone, let's have a toast to Billy Jo and Mark." He lifted his glass and clinked it with his spoon—and then the lights went out.

"Way to go, Danny. You knocked the lights out," Chris said as people murmured throughout the restaurant.

"Hey, let me check this out. I'll be right back," Mark said to Billy Jo, running his hand over her shoulder as he scraped back his chair.

"Guess there goes dinner," she said to him, sounding unusually calm. His dad was shining his phone, standing, and so was Chase.

Mark walked over to them, pulling his phone out and flicking on the flashlight.

"Likely the snowstorm," Jed said. The lights flicked

dimly on and then off again. The wind whistled faintly, and even in the darkness, Mark could see a full-blown snowstorm through all the windows.

He looked over to his dad. "Yeah, likely a line down…"

He started walking around tables to the front, where the waitstaff were lighting candles, right over to the dining room manager, Merv, who was behind the bar, barking out orders. Mark shook his head as he turned to his dad alongside him and said, "Snowstorm on the island could knock power out for days…" Then he dialed Carmen, who answered on the first ring.

"Hey, Chief. Power's out. Take it that's why you're calling."

He shook his head. "We just ordered dinner, and everything's gone dark. Here with my family…" Someone was talking in the background. "Are you at the office?"

"Yeah. Lacy just came back in, said all the lights are out in town. Ferry's been canceled the rest of the night because of the storm. The forecast isn't great. Seems this storm came out of nowhere and may not let up for a few days. Elisha is on the phone with utilities to find out more, but it's completely dark in town. Not sure how long it will take, with only one truck on the island. Could be a tree down over a line…" The phone rang in the background, and someone answered.

"Well, find out and call me," he said. "People start to panic and get scared. Keep your phone on and let me know what you find out."

He hung up and took in his dad and Chase, who were leaning against the bar, talking to Merv. He pulled his hand over his face as he strode over to them.

"Power's out to the entire island," said one of the waitstaff who had walked out from the back. He turned to Merv. "Turned the gas off, but we've got ten orders in queue and food on. What about the generator?"

Everyone was looking at Mark as if he were supposed to fix this.

"You know as much as I do," he said. "Lines are down and the power is out. Can you get the generator going, or are you going to close up?"

He had to think of what they had at home. The well needed power, and their generator needed gas, but at least there was the woodstove for heat. How much gas did he have? Maybe half a jerry can, because this wasn't something he'd been planning on.

"No, I'll get the generator on to finish the orders that are up," Merv said, "but we're not taking any more orders tonight. If anyone hasn't ordered, apologize and let them know. Hopefully the lines aren't down long." Then Merv was walking away back through the kitchen.

"Well, this kind of puts a damper on things," Chase said, gesturing to a waitress walking past with a tray of candles.

"What's the call time like here on the island?" Jed asked.

Mark shook his head. "Well, haven't been here that long, just over a year, but I've never been in a storm. Typically we have only one truck, and manpower has to come over from the mainland on the ferry. But I can tell you right now that with how bad the storm is, the ferry has been canceled for the night, so at the very least, it could be not till morning."

The lights flicked on, and a few people cheered. His dad reached over and tapped his shoulder. "Well, there's worse things. I'm sure we'll figure it out. If anything, it will be a great story to tell your kids, how a big storm hit right before your wedding."

Mark ran his hand over the back of his head as he looked over across the restaurant to where his family was waiting, talking, laughing. He shook his head. "Let's just hope they get the power back on, because a storm on the island takes up resources. When people get scared, holidays get canceled for first responders, and the chief of police could suddenly find his wedding being postponed."

Chase let his gaze linger on him, but Jed was shaking his head and said, "I don't think we're there yet. The power being out and the snowstorm aren't problems. Light some candles. As long as you have a minister, you can have a wedding."

All three of them looked over to the table, where Billy Jo was talking with his brothers. His family was there, and the last thing he wanted was to postpone anything, because Billy Jo wasn't the easy-going kind of girl who could just reschedule.

No, she was damn difficult. He realized it had likely been in a moment of weakness that he convinced her to accept a Christmas wedding, and he knew her well enough to know that likely would not happen a second time.

## Chapter 4

"How long you want to run the generator tonight?" Jed called out at the front door just as Chase shoved another piece of wood in the woodstove in the living room. Billy Jo still had her coat on, and she heard the stomping of feet as Mark appeared in his down coat as well, covered in snow. She pulled at her sweater, feeling uneasy. Everything seemed to be falling apart, and for a moment, she was plagued with the feeling that simple and easy weren't going to happen for her.

"I'm going to have to do a gas run," Mark said. "I used all the gas in the generator. Can you fill jugs so we have some water? Do what you need to, and I'll shut it off when I get back." He was standing right in front of her, and she felt Lucky brush her leg, his tail wagging.

"Yeah, I hate to say this, but if the power doesn't come back on, we may have to postpone the wedding," she said.

He just stared down at her, and she wasn't sure what to make of the flicker in his vibrant blue eyes. She knew he wouldn't listen. "Nope, not going there, and neither should you," he said. "Look, this is just a blip. We'll figure it out. My family's here, and so is yours. Power could come back on tonight or tomorrow. What's wrong?"

She heard voices in the background, but Mark hadn't moved, and she didn't want to argue over the fact that she was still reeling, unable to shake the feeling that she'd let down two kids and a family who didn't deserve any trouble. She made herself shake her head. "Nathan is furious with me. He may not have said it on the phone, but I could hear it in his voice. He blames me for Lisa showing up on his doorstep. I'm trying to help him get services, and I tried to explain to him that I didn't send her. The file we had was just to help him get some funding, some resources. I swear to Almighty God, the first chance I get to wrap my hands around Lisa's throat… I have half a mind to drive over to her place now, but lucky for her, a freak snowstorm has blanketed the island, and I wouldn't be able to see shit behind the wheel." She realized Mark's brothers were staring at her, and Mark wore an amused grin.

"Well, that's the spirit," he said. "Keep a positive outlook. But no to killing her. I will, though, happily look away for a second while you put the fear of God into her after we're married, after the honeymoon, when you're back. Unfortunately, as you've said, you can't do anything now, but in the meantime, you can fill some water while I get gas—if I can, with the power down."

Then Mark's cell phone was ringing, and he pulled it from his pocket. His brow knit. "It's Carmen," he said before he answered. "Hello? Yeah, okay, I'll head over there now." Then he hung up and leaned down to press a quick kiss to her lips. "Got to make another stop at the church. Doors are open, and Carmen can't get a hold of the minister. Likely some kids or someone."

"We'll tag along, maybe get a firsthand view of my little brother, the chief," Chris said. "And then you can drop us off at the hotel. J.D. and Evie said the hotel is turning the generator off at eleven."

Billy Jo reached down and brushed her hand over Lucky. "No, you get to stay home," she said to him, then watched as Mark headed out of the house with his two brothers.

"Diana, I'm going with Mark," Jed called out as well. "We're going to stop for some gas."

Billy Jo just listened to the footsteps of the men and the sound of the front door closing.

"I'm going to go get some more wood," her dad said, pulling on his coat.

Billy Jo turned to her mom and Diana.

"We should get some water jugs filled," Diana said, rubbing Billy Jo's arm.

"I'll grind some coffee for the morning in case the power is still out," her mom said.

"There are some big jugs in that far counter over there if you want to fill them up," Billy Jo said. "So sorry about this. Not exactly the comforts of home without power. You may wish you stayed at the hotel with Danny and Chris."

Diana and Jed were staying in one of the two bedrooms downstairs, her mom and dad in the other.

"Oh, don't be silly. This is fine," Diana said. "You have no idea the number of times we've lost power, living out of town on a well with septic. We learned fast to fill the bathtub when a storm was coming in. Always have water. You know, I can see how upset you are about those kids, and I'm going to tell you something. They're going to be okay. This is not an ideal situation, but they'll get through it. I grew up in foster care, I'm sure Mark told you, but I was one of the lucky ones. I had people who cared about me. I worked my way through school and became a lawyer so I could help people who need help.

"But I had a sister who died. She was severely disabled up here." Diana tapped her head. "Not really an official diagnosis. I grew up with nothing, with a mother who didn't care. To make a depressingly long story short, you can't put your life and happiness on hold. You did what you could, but you are not responsible for what Lisa did. You'll fix it when you get back, and those kids will get back with their parents, okay? This one is done. How many should we do?" Diana settled a big two-gallon jug of water on the island as her mom dumped freshly ground coffee into a plastic container.

"Just the three jugs. That's all we have," Billy Jo said.

Diana began filling another gallon jug as Billy Jo walked over to the cupboard and pulled out a half-gallon plastic juice carton.

"And this one," she added, holding it up as she walked over. "Mark didn't tell me you had a sister."

Diana didn't look at her. "I don't think I ever told him. Jed knows, of course, but it was something I never talked about with the kids. I didn't grow up in a loving home, but I made sure my boys were loved. Jed and I love them and our grandkids, and you know what?" She had filled the last jug, and she turned off the tap and faced her. "Even though it took me a long time to get past what I went through, I wouldn't be who I am if I didn't suffer the way I did. Those two kids, they'll be okay. I'm going to tell you this again, because there will be another two, and another, and you will do what you can, but you need to look after you."

Billy Jo realized Diana had shared something deeply personal, an old wound she hadn't even shared with Mark. "How am I supposed to get married and pretend everything is okay?"

Diana rested her palm on the island. Even Rose had stepped in closer to listen as she said, "You don't pretend. But let me ask you something. What are you going to accomplish by worrying? Can you speed up any of the process? Because I know well how the system works. A hearing is going to be set, and because of the holidays, nothing will happen until the new year. Reports and observations and recommendations still have to be filed by the doctor and the social worker, who is not you…" Diana said to her.

She couldn't believe how much Diana understood about how her job worked. "But I can call Grant, my boss, and his boss. I can demand, I can…" She didn't finish. Her mom and Diana were both watching her with a ton of sympathy. "Fine, you're right, I'll drive myself crazy, but what am I supposed to say to Nathan and Grace? They don't deserve this, and honestly, I can't blame him for his anger."

She heard the front door kick open.

"Okay, I stacked a bunch of wood," Chase called out. "It's really bad out there. I could barely see anything…" He walked right past her to the woodstove, and Diana and her mom looked back at her.

"You tell him the facts, how the process works, and what he can do," Diana said quite matter-of-factly.

"And you get married, and then you and Mark go on your honeymoon," her mom added.

"When you get back," Diana said, "the reports will be in, the hearing will be set, and you can go in with a clear head and be of more help to this family than you can be right now."

She knew Diana was right, but hearing it still didn't make her feel any better.

$$\text{————————————————}$$

# Chapter 5

$$\text{————————————————}$$

"You sure there's a road here?" Chris said from the back seat.

Mark couldn't remember ever driving in anything like this. His dad had rolled his window down and looked out as Mark gripped the wheel, slipping a few times even though his tires were good winter ones.

"How much farther?" Danny added from the back. "Shit, Mark, I can just make out a tree line. We go off the road, no one's going to find us."

"Both you two, knock it off," Jed said. "Mark, just stay in the middle of the road…"

The defrost was on full blast as the snow and icy chill from the open window swept in. He spotted what he thought was the sign to the church at the edge of town.

"It's right here," he said. "Geez, that sign is completely covered in snow."

The Jeep slid sideways as he turned down the driveway to the church and geared down, then steered into the skid, straightening the Jeep as he gave it some gas. The snow was piling up, and he stopped just as the church came into view.

"Maybe you should wait in the Jeep. I'll just be a minute," he said as he lifted his gaze to the rearview mirror and his brothers in back.

"Not a chance." Chris tapped the back of his head.

Mark turned off the Jeep as his dad stepped out. He opened his door and stepped out as well, then reached into his pocket for his flashlight and flicked it on, lifting his jacket just enough that his holstered sidearm was within reach. He could hear his brothers climbing out, the doors closing, and he trudged in his cowboy boots through the snow. He glanced once to his dad, who was looking around much like he was, and he listened to the wind and the crunch of snow beneath his feet. There were no other cars there, and he found himself squinting as a gust of wind and snow pelted his face.

He reached the steps and the snow that covered them and made his way up, hearing the footsteps behind him. "I don't see any tracks," he said as he reached the door, which was closed. *Weird.*

"What do you want to bet it was the minister?" Jed said.

He put his hand on the knob and expected it to be locked, but it pulled open. "Okay, didn't expect that," he said, shining his light inside the church, which was pitch black. His breath fogged in front of him as he stepped in.

"Hello, this is Chief Friessen! Anyone here?" he called out, hearing the squeak of the floorboards as his dad and brothers followed him inside. "Pull the door closed, Danny," he said. "That'll keep the snow out, at least. I'm just going to take a look around." He took in the pews, all stained dark wood, as he made his way up the aisle.

"So this is where you're saying 'I do'? Cute, but would be better with lights," Danny said, and he thought Chris grunted in response. His dad said nothing, but Mark knew he was right behind him.

He shone his light at the front of the church, landing on someone in the first pew, and his arm went out on instinct toward his dad.

"Hey, you okay in here? You need some help?" he called out. He took one step and then another, shining his flashlight. The person's coat hood was up, and he or she said nothing, leaning against the edge of the pew, not moving. He felt the slow, methodical pounding of his heart, and he pulled his gun on instinct.

"Answer me right now!" he called out. "Who are you? Dad, stay back."

He knew the person must have heard him. He took another step, seeing boots, blue jeans, and he tapped the foot, saying, "Come on, wake up. You can't be in here."

He shone the light right in the face and realized it was a woman, and her eyes were open. "Shit! Damn, fuck…" He holstered his gun and pulled back the hood to shine the light in her eyes. When he touched the side of her neck to feel for a heartbeat, he knew she was dead. "Okay, stay back," he called out. "This is a crime scene now."

His dad had his phone out with the flashlight on. "Is she dead?"

"Yeah." He looked back at the woman. Danny and Chris had joined them.

"She's young," Danny said, stepping toward him. "How old, do you think?"

He didn't want to guess. Twenty, maybe. He only shook his head and glanced over to his brother, wondering if he'd ever seen a body before. His dad hung back, and so did Chris.

"I don't know. This is…" He flashed his light around and pulled his phone out. "Come on, Danny, I'm serious. Get back. This is a crime scene, and with no lights here, you could be walking over all the evidence."

"How'd she die?" Chris asked. Jed glanced once to him and back over to the young lady.

Mark had his cell phone to his ear, listening to the ring. "I don't know. No lights, and I can't see any blood. Come on, Danny, seriously, get back."

"Hey, I could use your help," Carmen said immediately upon answering. "The phone lines have gone down now, but cell towers are working. Power crew said several power poles are down, and they can't get any more over until the ferry is running again, but until this storm lets up, it's not going to. I've got people coming into the station, five seniors saying they have electric heat only. I talked with the firehouse and ambulance, and they're going to set up a warming center at the station, where they have a generator running—"

He shut his eyes. "Carmen, I get it. Listen, I'm at the church. You said someone called in that the door was open. Who called? Because I'm here now, and the door was closed but unlocked, and there's the body of a woman here. She's dead."

There was silence for a second.

"I don't know who it was," Carmen replied. "Lacy took the call. Just said the door was open. Do you know who it is?"

He shook his head. His dad was still shining a light

on the young woman. "No idea. Never seen her before. Look, get Elisha to hold down the station. I need you out here at the church. Call the coroner, too, and pick him up if you can. The roads are bad. Visibility is zero, and the snow is piling up. And I need you to get me the number for the minister."

He thought he heard Carmen swear under her breath. He thought of Kyle Drake, the old minister, who, according to Gail Shephard, had been with the church since her kids were born.

"I'll have Lacy call you with his number," she said.

He angled his head to where his dad was shining the light. "Okay, call me right back," he said, then hung up.

"Mark, look at her right hand," Jed said.

He shoved his phone in his pocket and walked over to the body, then squatted down, flicking his flashlight on the small hand, which appeared to be clutching a piece of paper.

"Well, what does it say?" Danny asked.

Mark glanced back to his brother and shone a light right in his eyes. "Geez, Danny, I don't know. It's still in her hand—you know, evidence? You're a lawyer. What do you think a good defense lawyer would do with all this? She's dead. There could be prints on the note, and I have no gloves."

A small Kleenex package landed on the floor in front of him. "Here, use a Kleenex," Chris said. Mark reached for it.

"You carry Kleenex around in your pocket?" Danny said.

"J.D. put it there. You telling me your wife doesn't?" Chris said right back.

Mark pulled out a Kleenex and heard the floor creak

behind him as his dad stepped closer, shining the light on the hand. He used a Kleenex to pull out the paper, seeing it was a note, and he stood and tucked his flashlight in his pocket.

"What does it say?" Danny asked again.

"Let Mark do his job, you two," his dad finally cut in.

Mark used the Kleenex to unfold the paper, and he took in a list of names—all members of his family. At the top, in all bold, was the word **KILL**, and listed below were the names of everyone he loved, including Billy Jo, his parents, his brothers, their wives, and his two nieces.

"Those are our names," he heard Danny say, and he looked over his shoulder to see his dad and brothers standing right there, everyone staring at the names on the list that had been in the hand of a dead woman in a church on the eve of his wedding.

"Yeah," Mark said.

"A kill list?" Chris said.

"It is," was all he could get out, his heart thumping long and loud.

His dad rested his hand on his shoulder as he said, "Lord Almighty, son, just what the hell did you do?"

## Chapter 6

The sound of his breath echoed as he stared at the word *kill*, and he dropped the note, an icy chill running up his spine. His gun was out.

"Down!" he shouted as he flashed his light, but his brothers and his dad just stood there, looking around. He gestured to them, because they were targets, and said, "Dad, move! Get down over there."

He took in the dead woman and moved to the front of the church. "Who's here? Come out now!" He shone his flashlight, seeing nothing but an empty church, and turned back to see his dad flashing his light the other way, looking around.

"Don't see anyone in here," Chris said.

Mark shone his light down each of the pews as he walked to the front of the church. "Just stay down and out of the way until I have a chance to look around," he whispered loudly as he stepped up behind the lectern, glancing to the back of the church. Then he moved to the back door, keeping his back to the wall. He reached for the knob and turned, then shoved the door open and let it smack the wall as he spun around, gun and light up.

"Show yourself! This is Chief Friessen. Come out! I will shoot." He was loud as he shone his light in the back room, his breath fogging from the cold and his heart pounding loud and long in his ears. He did a sweep of the back, pulling open a closet but seeing just coats and some stacked boxes, then moved over to the exit, which was locked. He stepped back out into the small church, seeing Danny crouched now, holding the letter and shining his phone flashlight on it.

"See anyone?" Mark called out as he made his way down the side, shining his light into all the pews to the front door. He opened it to see a full-on storm, the wind whistling. He could just hear his dad and brothers talking as he pulled the door closed and locked it before walking back up the aisle.

"No one," Jed said. "You have any idea who this is, son?"

Mark wished for lights, anything to be able to see, as he shone his flashlight back on the woman. Her eyes were open and sightless, her face was pale, and her hair, from what he could make out, was brown. Her boots had no snow on them, and her hands were bare. The floor was wet, but he realized that could have been from them.

"Never seen her before," he said.

Why the list? Damn, it seemed for a moment as if he always had a target on him.

"Give me your keys," Chris said. It was dark, but he could see his breath fog. Chris was in his face now with his phone flashlight. "I'm going back to the hotel. My wife and kids are not safe. They're on a list in a dead woman's hand. What the hell are you involved in here, Mark?" His voice was accusing, and his hand thumped his chest.

Danny had his cell phone to his ear and was now standing, still holding the note, as he said, "Evie, you and J.D. need to get the girls dressed. No, no, no…" It was a one-sided conversation.

Mark reached into his pocket and pulled out his keys, which Chris took. "I have no idea, Chris. Seriously, you think I would put you all in danger? Go pick up everyone. I'll have Elisha meet you at the hotel. Move everyone to my place. I'll call Billy Jo…"

"No, do not open the door to anyone until Chris and I get there," Danny continued, his voice urgent. "Just listen to me. I'll explain when I see you."

"Mark, listen, son," Jed said. "That list has all our names on it. I think we need to all go. Mark, you got some guns at home?"

Mark thought of the gun box in his closet with his spare sidearm and the arsenal of shotguns at the station. "This is an active crime scene. I can't leave. But go with them, Dad. I've got Carmen on her way…"

"I'm not leaving you here alone," Jed said. "Danny, Chris, you go. I'll call your mom and tell her you're coming."

Mark watched as his brothers started to the front of the church.

Danny flicked open the lock and turned back. "Lock this up after us. Mark, what have you got for ammo, guns?"

"I have a sidearm at home. I'll stop at the station to pick up some shotguns and ammo. This could mean nothing," he started as he followed his brothers to the door. When they opened it, the wind nearly ripped it from Danny's hand. "Call me from the hotel."

Chris reached out and squeezed his shoulder. "I know this is your job, little brother, but don't stay long. You have too many things working against you—a snowstorm, no power, and that list."

He could see the anger and the worry in his brother. "Just go and get everyone," he said, then reached for the door.

His brothers made their way down and over to his Jeep just as he made out lights and heard the spinning of tires. Damn, that had to be Carmen. He stepped out and lifted his hand to try to see. His Jeep was backing out, its headlights on, its tires spinning in the deep snow, and then he spotted Carmen trudging toward him with her flashlight.

"Where's the coroner?" he shouted as she moved closer and up the steps in her dark jacket, a winter hat pulled over her dark hair, shaking her head.

"He's gone off island and is stuck on the other side until after the storm." She had her hand on the door, and Mark stepped inside. Carmen followed, and he reached for his phone as she pulled the door closed, shining her flashlight. "You said there's a body? Who is it? Any idea what happened?

He was walking up the center aisle with her toward where Jed was standing, one hand in his pocket, the other shining a light on the body, staring. Mark gestured to him. "That's my dad, Jed Friessen. Dad, this is Carmen, a detective." He stopped in front of the body. "You have an evidence bag? Because in her hand was that note."

Carmen pulled a bag from her pocket and reached

for the note, which was sitting on the bench with the Kleenex.

"It lists everyone in my family, a kill list," he continued. She flicked her gaze up to him, but in the dark, it was hard to make out. Mark dialed his phone, and it rang once.

"Yes, Chief?"

"Elisha, I need you to get over to my nieces and sisters-in-law, Evie and J.D., at the hotel. My brothers have my Jeep and are on their way over. I need you to help get them out of there and over to my place. I'm at the church now, and there's the body of a woman here, and she had a list in her hand with the names of my family under the word *kill*."

"Seriously, Chief?" Elisha replied.

Mark shook his head, hearing his dad say something in a low voice to Carmen. "Yeah, and I need you to stay at my house until I get back."

"Okay, Chief, on my way."

"Wait, are you at the station?" He didn't know what he heard in the background.

"Yeah. A few of the residents are here. I was going to move over to the firehall. Lacy is here, too."

He shook his head but knew she couldn't see him. "Just leave them. Tell Lacy to lock the doors. I want you to load up three of the shotguns and bring them with you, and some of the gear. Grab my vest, too."

"Got it," she said. "You think we have a killer on the island? Is this for real?"

He didn't know what to say, considering the wedding was a day away and he had a target on him. "Can only assume it is. Call me as soon as you get to the hotel," he said, then hung up and turned back to his dad and Carmen.

"I called your mom and filled her in," his dad said.

He realized Carmen was taking photos of the body just as his phone started ringing. The caller ID was home, and he pressed the green answer icon. "Hello?"

"Where are you, and what's going on? Your mom said Danny and Chris are moving everyone over here?" Billy Jo never sounded worried, but there was an edge in her voice.

"I'll tell you when I get there. We won't be long. Not much we'll be able to do here tonight. Look, Elisha is coming too and will stay at the house until I get there. I want you to go and get my gun from the lockbox in the bedroom and keep it with you. Stay in the house. Don't answer the door."

"Mark, what the hell is going on?"

He shook his head and let out a heavy sigh as he turned back, taking in Carmen and his dad again. "There's a woman dead in the church, and she had a note in her hand with *kill* written at the top, then your name and the names of everyone in my family."

There was silence. Then she said, "Okay, hurry home, please—and, Mark, be careful."

He would have smiled if things weren't so dire. "Yeah, love you," he said, then hung up and pocketed his phone, feeling his gun. He looked down to the body. Carmen was searching her empty pockets and unzipping her coat. She shook her head.

"She has no ID, Chief. I have no idea who she is. What do you want to do? We got a storm that could only get worse, and no lights. This body isn't going anywhere."

This wasn't supposed to be happening. He let out a heavy sigh again. "We'll leave her and come back, I guess."

"You want to cover up the body at least, son?" his dad said.

Mark shook his head. "No, better not contaminate the crime scene more than we already have. Carmen, can you get prints on your phone?"

She already had her phone out, and Mark reached for her flashlight. "Yeah, and I'll get a close-up of her face and send it off to the lab. Maybe we can get an ID tonight since the cell towers are still working." She fingerprinted the thumb and fingers with the scanner from her phone.

Mark felt a tap on his shoulder from his dad, who gestured to him and said, "Mark, you didn't answer me before, but I can only imagine, with you doing the job you do, that you've made yourself some enemies. Whoever it is, Mark, they hate you enough that they did their homework and looked into our family—us, my granddaughters, your brothers, Evie and J.D., and Billy Jo. You have no idea who it is?"

Why did he feel as if his dad didn't believe him? He thought of why he'd had to leave North Lakewood and the sheriff's department there. "I can guess, but I don't know for sure, Dad. An angry spouse, someone I put away? With the toes I've stepped on, could be a long or short list."

His dad nodded and rested a hand on his shoulder. "Well, let's get out of here. I think I'll feel better when we're back at your place and everyone is under one roof." He shook his head again. "But when we get back there, I want you to sit down and make a list of everyone."

"Dad, I'm the cop here."

His dad smiled. "And I'm still your father, Mark. Just remember that."

## Chapter 7

Mark heard his family's voices as he pressed bullets into the spare clip for his sidearm. The battery-operated lantern on the bedside table gave off just enough light, considering the generator was now off and the spare empty gas can in the back of the Jeep would have to wait until the sun came up. He had completely forgotten about it.

He felt the hand on his back and would know her touch anywhere.

"You okay?" Billy Jo stepped around him, her arm around his waist, leaning against him. Damn, she felt so good, and he realized she was the only one he knew would never blame him.

"My brothers are furious with me," he said. "I've basically put a target on all of them, on you, on my mom and dad. I don't know what sick fuck did this. And now my dad is treating me like a kid, wanting me to sit and make a list of people who have an ax to grind with me, but I have no idea where to start and no clue why now. If I'd had any idea being a cop would put a target on my family…"

"You'd, what, not have become a cop?" She sounded so calm and reasonable. "But you're okay with a target on yourself?"

He glanced down at her in the dim light and just squeezed the clip, then slid his other arm around her, pulling her closer and kissing the top of her head.

"Don't answer that," she said. "I can see it in your face, in your expression. With your family, you don't quite fit—but at the same time, you do. You were born to be a cop, and it's not your fault some crazy dead person just happened to write down some names. For all you know, it was just her, and no one else is coming after us. It could be something as simple as an angry psychopath wanting nothing more than to fuck with your head. Do I need to point out that you have an arsenal out there? Your dad, Chris, and Danny have a shotgun and are taking turns keeping watch, so to speak, and your dad and mine double-checked every window to make sure everything is locked. Just FYI, your brothers are not angry at you. It's the situation. They're scared more than anything."

What was it about Billy Jo? She knew the right thing to say to make him feel better, and he valued her perspective.

"We're supposed to be getting married," he said. "Instead we have no power, a snowstorm, and everyone crowded in our house. I never told them why I really had to leave my job in North Lakewood. Is something always going to follow me, haunt me?"

She didn't say anything at first. Then Mark felt the weight in his chest as she slid her hand over it and just rested it there. "You thinking they're sending a message to you? Maybe it's time your family knew."

She stepped around right in front of him, sliding her hands over his chest, and he slid his fingers over her cheek and tucked her shoulder-length brown hair behind her ears. How would he get his family to understand the horror of finding that note in Sophie's backpack, a warning from a dirty cop, all because Mark hadn't been willing to look away?

There was a tap on the open bedroom door.

"Sorry to interrupt, Mark," Jed said. "We have Ally and Sophie set up in our room. Diana is getting them settled on an air mattress on the floor. All is quiet. You put any thought into who wants to come after you?"

Billy Jo was still touching him as he turned around, tucking the clip in the pouch beside his holstered gun.

"Sure," he said. "It could be a lot of people, but Carmen has the prints, and once we ID that woman, it will tell me a lot more than what I have now."

He knew Billy Jo was right there, and she settled her hand over his arm. It was just a touch, but as he looked down to her, even though it was dim, he knew she was there for him.

"I never told you why I left and came here," he finally said. He didn't have to look at his dad to know he was confused, as he felt the nudge beside him.

"You need to tell them, Mark."

"Yes, I think you'd better tell us," Jed said. "Come on, son."

Billy Jo slid her hand in his as he reached for the lantern and started walking out. The flickering wood-stove and lit candles heating the house gave off a faint light in the living room. He spotted Chris to the right, holding a shotgun. He knew the safety was on. That was just something his dad had taught them about how to care for and use a gun safely, everything by the time they were twelve. Mark set the lantern on the island and glanced once to Billy Jo, who was standing beside him.

"Well?" his dad said.

J.D., tall and slender, her long hair pulled back, had walked in and over to Chris, and she asked, "What's going on?"

"I don't know," was all Chris said.

Mark took in his mom, Evie, Rose, Chase, and Danny, then looked down at Billy Jo again. He was front and center and under the kind of spotlight he didn't want.

"I never told any of you why I really left North Lakewood and the sheriff's office—well, not the real story."

"Does it have something to do with that list? Is someone coming after us because of you?" Danny cut in, angry. "What the hell did you do, brother?"

"Hey, you need to give Mark a minute to tell you what happened," Billy Jo said. "The fact is that your brother wouldn't stay silent about some dirty cops, so with all due respect, Danny, don't go blaming Mark because he has some integrity. I get that you're angry and scared, but don't direct that at your brother."

He couldn't pull his gaze from Billy Jo. She wanted to fight for him. He hadn't expected that.

"Dirty cops? What is this about, son?" Jed cut in. Chase had stepped closer, right behind Rose, narrowing his gaze shrewdly.

"The reason I left North Lakewood, the reason I no longer had a job as a deputy there, was because a code of silence was protecting some dirty cops. During a shakedown, they planted evidence, made false arrests. I arrived on the scene to see a man cuffed and bleeding facedown on the ground. You know when someone has been beaten.

"The two deputies were neck deep in something, trying to get their stories straight. Said he was stealing, a drifter, that he attacked them, that he died en route to the hospital. It turned out he worked at the location as a hired hand. They told me to leave, said they'd handle it, but I knew they were lying, so I refused. I'd kept notes, journals, after taking a complaint to the sheriff once and being told to drop it. I started investigating them myself, and when I had enough and knew even the sheriff had to go, I took the file to the Feds, believing they would be all over it.

"Only they circled the wagons. Seems whistleblowers are very unpopular and often have accidents or suddenly commit suicide. I realized going against that blue wall was going to be the end of me. I was suddenly hated by every cop in three counties, which told me the Feds had shared everything and sold me out. The day the sheriff called me into his office and asked for my badge, he said he was doing it for my own good, because the way things were going, he'd be on your doorstep and I'd be in a pine box."

His mom gasped, and suddenly it was so quiet.

"But it didn't end there," he continued. "A file was on the sheriff's desk, a thick file filled with complaints about me signed by fictional complainants, I think, or they could have been coerced, for all I know, by the cops who hated me or any one of their informants, people in the area who had never been up to any good. I was forced out, unprotected. Dad, you remember your horse, Parsons, who was poisoned?"

Jed didn't pull his gaze from Mark. "Are you saying that was a message to you from one of the deputies in our hometown?" He sounded unusually calm, but Mark knew his dad well enough to know he was anything but.

"It wasn't just the horse," Mark said. "Then my tires were slashed in town, and then Sophie found a note in her backpack. She came home from school and handed it to me. She didn't know how it had gotten there, but it was a message that they could get to me through my family anytime and in any way they wanted…"

"In my daughter's backpack? Who put it there?" Chris was far calmer than Danny, but Mark could see he was ready to kill someone.

"I don't know. She found it at school. The message was received, and that was why I left. The only problem was that no one would hire me, so the only options I had were Alaska or here. Tolly Shephard hired me knowing the baggage I had, what I'd done or tried to do. Chris, I have no idea if it was one of the deputies, their family, or someone they hired…"

His family was suddenly very quiet. What they were thinking, he didn't know.

"You should have told us, Mark," Diana said. "We could have gone after them and done something…"

Jed glanced over to her. Danny had lifted his hands and linked them behind his head, and Evie appeared shellshocked in the candlelight.

"You did the right thing, Mark," Chase said. "You wouldn't have won. You're right that the message was to scare you. Next, they could have killed someone. Moving on the way you did took the target off your family. But, Mark, I have to say that while finding a body holding a list of names of your family seems personal, I think it's the wrong kind of personal."

The way Chase said it had him realizing how much Billy Jo's father really understood about the law. "I agree, but I can't rule anything out."

"Mark, you should have told us anyway," Danny said, gesturing. "The fact is that a target was on us, and maybe it still could be."

Chris was shaking his head. "Seriously, you can be a dumbass sometimes."

"Your brothers are right, Mark," Jed said. "You should have said something. I won't stand for my son being chased out of our home. When we get back, Sheriff Joffe and I will be having a heart to heart. I won't be bullied or have any of my family threatened. I will bring him and his department down."

He knew his dad meant it, but he didn't want a target on his family. "I get it, Dad, but Chase is right. There were too many bad actors in power. You want that out, you vote it out. Get a new sheriff in there, someone with integrity, honesty. You've got to start at the local level…"

He knew his dad was frustrated by the way he ran his hand over his short hair, which was turning a nice shade of gray. "You know what? I hear you, Mark, and once we settle this, I think we need to sit down and talk about that. But something has bothered me since we walked into that church. The door was unlocked. What about the minister?" His dad gestured to him.

Mark knew he was frowning. Maybe it was his silence that had Billy Jo sliding her hand over his lower back.

"Mark, have you talked to the minister?" she said as she looked up at him.

"Nope. Kind of had my focus elsewhere. I asked Carmen to get me his number…" He pulled his cell phone from his pocket, seeing nothing from Carmen, so he dialed her number. Everyone was quiet and watching him. It rang once, twice.

"Chief, we got another problem," she said on answering. The wind whistled in the background.

He turned and gave everyone his back as he took in Lucky in his dog bed. The knot in his chest, which seemed to be his constant companion, tightened. "Tell me," he said, hearing the whispers of his family behind him.

"The minister, Kyle Drake?" Carmen said. "Well, he's dead."

---

## Chapter 8

---

Mark put on his heavy winter coat and laced up his boots. This was the first time Billy Jo had ever seen him wear anything other than cowboy boots. She was still trying to wrap her head around what he had said. Kyle Drake, the old guy who was supposed to marry them, was dead.

She reached for her dusty rose down coat in the closet after changing into thick socks, a warm sweatshirt of Mark's, and blue jeans.

"What are you doing?" Mark said. She heard footsteps in the hall and glanced over. The soft light from the battery-operated lantern shone on Chris, still holding a shotgun, and Jed behind him.

"I'm going with you." She shoved her arms into her coat.

"No, you're not," he said. "You stay here. There's a storm out there, and I have no idea what the hell I'm walking into. The last thing I need to be worried about is you. We have two bodies now, the power is out, and we're cut off from the mainland."

Chris handed the shotgun to Jed and stepped around Mark, who had lifted his foot onto the bench to tie his other boot. Billy Jo could just make out the boots she never wore in the back of the closet, and she pulled them out and moved over for Chris, who had on his heavy coat and pulled on his boots too, saying nothing.

"No, I'm not staying," she said. "I'm not some helpless female who needs to hide out here, Mark. You have a body and have no idea who she is. She was holding a list with all our names on it, so this is personal. And now the minister is dead? Yeah, no. I'm coming."

Mark was shaking his head. She wondered if Jed or Chris would add his two cents. She really didn't know Mark's family well.

"Billy Jo, Mark is right," Chase said from where he stood behind Jed, her mom with him. "You shouldn't be out there."

"Well, neither should Mark. I see you're willing to take Chris, though. Please tell me this isn't because you think I can't look after myself. Mark, you know I've never sat home on the sidelines, and I'm not about to start now."

He was shaking his head, taking one step and then another until he stood in front of her. He was so tall. She knew he didn't want to argue, but she knew too when he was digging his heels in.

"Please," he said. "The last thing I need to worry about out there is you, Billy Jo. I don't have any idea what this is about, if I did something that has someone coming after you again. So please, please, for me, I beg you, please stay here."

She'd do anything for him. She really loved him. "Then you'll stay too?"

He swore under his breath and ran his hand over his head before reaching for a hat and pulling it on. "Fine," he said. "But you stay out of the way and go where I tell you to."

She had never expected it to be that easy. She reached into the closet for a wool hat and gloves. "I promise," she said as Mark pulled open the front door, taking the shotgun from Jed.

He gestured to Chris and said, "Let's go."

She followed Mark's brother out the front door and took in her car, which was buried in snow, as they made their way over to the Jeep. Chris had a flashlight, and she felt Mark's hand on her back.

"Get in the back," he said to her and opened his driver's door. Billy Jo climbed into the back seat, and Mark set the shotgun on the floor at her feet. He started the Jeep, and Chris was already brushing the snow off the windshield. Mark turned in the seat to face her.

"I love you, Billy Jo, but you have to let me do my job."

Maybe it was the way he said it, but she wondered for a moment if this was what it would be like, being married to Mark. "I have never not let you do your job. Don't coddle me. I'm not helpless. We are not married yet, Mark, and I hope you're not thinking that putting a ring on my finger gives you the right to tell me what I can and can't do or expect me to stay home and wait for you patiently. If you think I'm going to do whatever you say, you have the wrong girl."

The door closed, and they both glanced over to Chris, who was looking at them. She wasn't sure what to make of his expression. Of course, he'd heard everything.

"You two done arguing?" he said. "We should go. If it's all the same to you, I'd rather not be sitting out here with, for all we know, some madman on the loose."

Billy Jo sat back, reached for her seatbelt, and pulled it on as Mark shoved the Jeep in gear and spun around in the snow. His wiper blades were going full out, back and forth, but all she could see was thick heavy snow blowing only a foot in front of them. He skidded a few times as he turned in silence down a side road before the church. She had her hand on the back of his seat.

"Can't see a damn thing out here," Chris said.

Mark only grunted, then slowed and rolled down his window. She didn't know how he could see anything. He backed up, and she could hear the spinning of his tires as he pulled down what she thought was a driveway. He pulled up beside the sheriff's cruiser, and she could just make out a house. Mark looked back once to her after he turned off the vehicle, and Chris opened his door and the inside light popped on.

"Stay close," Mark said to her as he turned around in his seat. His gaze lingered, and the stubbornness she'd never been able to shake gave way. She saw something she'd never seen in him before: fear.

He stepped out before she could say anything, then reached for the shotgun on the floor before moving the seat forward and helping her out. He closed the door and then touched her back as he started walking and said, "Come on."

Chris had a flashlight shining and the front door opened, and she spotted Carmen, a light on inside the small house.

"In here," Carmen said.

Billy Jo stepped back as Chris went in first, brushing

snow off him. She followed into a small entrance. A lamp was on inside, and Mark closed the door behind her. Carmen stood in a small living room, in which she could just make out a side chair and table and a lamp, listening to the creak of the floor.

"Show me what you found," Mark said.

Billy Jo hung back with Chris, who was looking around, shining a flashlight at the framed photos on the wall, family or something. She stepped forward but froze as she took in the dead body of the minister. His glasses were smashed, and she realized she had gasped, as Mark and Carmen were looking at her. She forced herself to swallow. The body was lying on the floor in what she thought was blood.

"What happened to him?" she asked.

Mark was looking at her, then back to the body. "Looks like he was stabbed. Carmen, you find a knife?"

"Already bagged it up," she said. "Put it in the trunk for evidence. From what I can see, he's been stabbed at least ten times. Whoever did this was angry. See the leg? They stabbed him there and in the chest, stomach, and arm. But I want to show you something else."

Billy Jo was still staring at the body.

"What is it?" Mark said in that way of his that was all cop. She realized how much he really had on his plate as he followed Carmen into the small dining room.

"I found something here while I was waiting for you," she said. "Under the table, look at the rug. What does that look like to you?"

Billy Jo was following as Mark pulled out a flashlight from Carmen and set the shotgun on the floor. An old green and brown rug was caught on something—a trap door?

"Is that what I think it is?" Mark pulled the rug back, and even she could see the cutout and the latch.

"A door to a basement or something covered by a rug under a dining table," Carmen said. "Seems he's hiding something."

Mark stood up, still holding the flashlight. "Help me with this table, Chris."

Chris walked around Carmen and took one end of the table, and Mark lifted the other and moved it over. "It could be a cold cellar too. Some of these old houses have that," Chris added.

Mark said nothing as he looked at his brother and then over to her.

Carmen reached for the handle and lifted the door, and Mark shone a light down as she said, "There's a ladder, but can't see for sure what's down here."

He went down on his knees and looked down. "Hello? This is Chief Friessen. Anyone down there?"

She didn't know what she expected. Maybe that was why her heart was thudding.

"What are you doing?" Carmen said as Mark stepped down and onto the ladder, holding his flashlight and lifting his jacket to pull out his gun.

"Going down and having a look. Shine the other light down here."

Billy Jo took another step closer and realized her hands were sweating. There was just something off about the hole Mark was climbing into. She willed for him to be okay.

"Mark, what's down there?" Chris called out. She couldn't see him anymore after he stepped off the ladder, and she heard him stumble and swear.

"Mark!" She knew she sounded panicked, but he

wasn't answering. She looked over to Carmen. Then a light appeared from below. "Are you okay?" she called out. The light was blinding her.

"Fine, just stumbled. There are rooms down here, bedrooms, doors with locks, and boxes stacked. There's a fax machine, too…" Then he said nothing, and she waited for him to climb back up, but instead he continued. "I'm not sure the crime scene is just upstairs. What I'm seeing down here is giving me a picture that Kyle Drake may have been doing something a minister shouldn't be doing."

For just a second, as the light Chris was holding flickered on Mark, she could see the weight of everything he carried. "So what do you want to do, Mark?" she said.

He looked up to her, and she realized there was likely something there he didn't want her to see. He shook his head, so she knelt down and put her foot on the ladder.

"What are you doing, Billy Jo?" he called out. "No, don't come down here."

But she was already climbing down, all the way down. She felt his hand touch her as she stepped into something dank and dark, and a strange feeling came over her. "I know you, Mark, and that look on your face. You found something."

He said nothing but winced, and she slid her hand over his, which was holding the flashlight, and shone it down a hall of concrete and padlocked plywood doors. There it was, the knot again, that sick feeling she'd known as a kid.

He stood behind her and slid his arm around her, pulling her close to him, and he shone the light to the corner, where there was an old teddy bear and children's shoes and clothes, then up the concrete wall, where an empty shackle hung.

"Mark…" That was all she could get out.

"I know," he said, not letting her go.

Billy Jo couldn't pull her eyes from what she was seeing, and now she knew why that sick feeling wouldn't leave her. Kyle Drake, who was supposed to marry her and Mark, wasn't a good man or a man of God. He was a monster.

## Chapter 9

There wasn't a chance Mark was going to be able to make Billy Jo leave. She stood there, and he was still trying to get his head around what he was seeing. She took his flashlight from his hand and stepped closer to the clothes on the cement floor.

"Billy Jo, don't touch," was all he said to her as he glanced over to the ladder, seeing the light his brother was shining down.

"What's going on, Mark?" Chris called out, and for a second he didn't know if he could find the words.

"I need some light down here," he said. "There are some kids' clothes and locked doors, a kind of dungeon or something. I don't know what the hell Kyle was up to. There seems to be tunneling. I see padlocks on doors…"

"Mark, take this flashlight, and I'll see if I can find a generator," Chris said, holding down the big flashlight that threw off more light. Mark stepped up on the bottom rung of the ladder and reached for it, seeing Carmen still leaning there in the opening.

"Chris, keep that shotgun with you," Mark said.

"Whoever did this could be somewhere on the property. Carmen, go with my brother, and call Elisha too. Snowstorm or not, I need her out here."

"You got it, Chief," Carmen said as she pushed away from the edge.

Mark stepped off the ladder, shining the flashlight toward Billy Jo, who was squatting by the clothes. He listened to the footsteps above him and realized someone could hear everything down there. Billy Jo glanced back to him and stood up, and he realized it was warmer down there, too. His breath didn't fog.

"A T-shirt and pants from a very young kid…" She rubbed her brow roughly.

Mark walked over, pulled out his pocketknife, and squatted down. He used it to lift a corner of the shirt to see how small it was, then the blue pants with what looked like blood on the leg. That sick feeling always came over him when he thought of crimes against children. Why? How could this be happening on his island?

"What do you think from the size of the clothes? Maybe a five-, six-year-old?" he said, then glanced back to Billy Jo, who was dragging the small flashlight over the built-in against the wall behind them.

She had her back to him, and he wasn't sure she was listening until she said, "Or a small seven- or eight-year-old." She sounded unusually calm, looking at a wall of cupboards, a counter, and a hallway.

He stood up, strode over to her, and tapped her back. "I'm going to have a look around. You okay?" he said. It was dark, but he could still make out the grimness that lingered and the heaviness in her eyes.

"You mean aside from the fact that we're standing in what appears to be a secret dungeon in the home of the minister who was going to marry us? He's been on the island for decades, yet he seems to be the devil himself, doing God knows what kinds of nefarious things to kids." Sarcasm dripped from her voice, but he knew that was how she sounded when she was scared. "See the fax machine, piles of paper…?" She shone her flashlight at the treasure trove. "Wonder if the way he was stabbed up there has anything to do with what he was doing down here?"

Yeah, he'd already figured that much out.

"Stay back, okay?" he said. "Let me have a look around."

She was shining her light, looking around, and then dragged her gaze back up to him and shook her head. She didn't have to say anything. He felt how sick all of this was as he took in the hallway and the plywood doors, the hinges, the cracked-open padlocks sitting on hooks. He shone his light down the hall, which didn't go as deep as he'd thought. There were four doors, two on each side.

The lights popped on, and he looked up and turned to see surprise on Billy Jo's face.

"Either the power's back on or they found a generator," Mark said. He heard a door clatter shut and footsteps on the floor above him.

"Mark, we found a generator in the shed out back," Chris shouted. Then he poked his head down and frowned. "What the hell…?"

Chris started down the ladder, and Carmen followed him.

Mark pulled open one of the plywood doors to see darkness beyond. He glanced at Carmen and said, "Check all the other doors." Then he shone his flashlight in. On a cot in the corner, a blanket was tossed in a heap. There was a plate on the floor with crumbs, and a bucket sat in the corner. On the wall outside the door, he spotted a switch. When he flicked it, a single bulb popped on in the room. It was maybe eight by ten, with a cement floor and Styrofoam on the wall and ceiling.

He heard something behind him and glanced back to see his brother. The look on his face was like nothing he'd ever seen before. He heard Carmen rattling the other doors.

"Was he keeping kids down here?" Chris said. "Billy Jo said those were a little kid's clothes out there. Good God, Mark, what is this? What was this guy doing?"

He didn't want to answer. What was he supposed to say? He looked back to his brother. "Do I need to spell it out to you? Whatever it was, it was sick, twisted, fucked up, but I likely don't even know the half of it," he said under his breath.

As he stepped into the tiny room, his hair brushed the Styrofoam ceiling, and he hunched over, feeling how close it was. It was nothing more than a box. The cot wouldn't fit an adult, and even with the thin blanket, it wasn't that warm.

"Chief, you'd better come down here and see this," Carmen called out.

Mark was relieved to step out. He knew he'd never get this sick hidden place out of his mind. Chris was staring past him into the tiny boxlike room. Then he looked right at him but said nothing.

Mark flicked off his flashlight. Carmen and Billy Jo were at the end of the hall. All the doors were open, and the one across was identical, another box with a cot. He wiped the back of his hand over his nose, fighting a lingering odor, likely from what was in the buckets. Every step he took, an anger he couldn't remember ever feeling built inside him.

He stopped where Billy Jo and Carmen were standing in the doorway. "What is it?"

Both were staring into the room, where the light was on. Carmen was looking right at him, wide eyed, and she just shook her head. Then Billy Jo stepped into the room slowly, and all he saw was the child on the floor in the corner.

"It's okay," Billy Jo said, crouching down. "What's your name, honey?"

The child was dirty and young, four, five, or six, and scared, wearing just an oversized T-shirt. Mark glanced at Carmen.

"I'll call an ambulance," she said, then brushed out past his brother, who was suddenly there. Mark looked back to where Billy Jo was still crouched before the child, who said nothing.

"Billy Jo, how is she—he?" Mark couldn't tell if it was a boy or girl.

She didn't look back at him. "A little boy, Mark. He's tiny. I'm guessing three or four." She was unzipping her coat and pulled it off, then sat on the concrete floor. The bucket had been spilled, and he flinched at the smell. He looked back at his brother.

"You look cold," Billy Jo said. "Do you want to put my coat on? It's okay. I won't hurt you. My name is Billy Jo, and that big guy back there is Mark. He's a police chief, and we're here to help you."

His heart was thudding as Billy Jo glanced back at him. The child was scared—no, terrified. He had to remind himself to breathe easy, no sudden moves. Chris was right there beside him now.

"Mark, that's a little kid, for the love of God," he said under his breath.

"Billy Jo," Mark called out again, amazed at the way she kept her energy even. "What can I do?"

She looked over to him and just shook her head. "It's okay. What's your name, honey? Can you hold up your fingers and tell me how old you are?"

He didn't know how she'd done it, but she had slipped her coat around the small child. Mark stepped into the room, crouching from the low ceiling, and took in how wide the child's eyes were the closer he got. He had started whining, terrified of him, so he stopped. Somehow Billy Jo managed to slide her arm around him.

"It's okay," she said. "Mark is a good guy. He won't hurt you. I won't hurt you." She was nodding to the child, and he knew it was a little boy the more he looked at him.

"I don't belong here," the child said.

Mark felt his eyes dampen, burning, and he blinked. He didn't cry, but this was something he'd never seen before, not like this.

"We're here to get you out of here. Can you tell me your name? How old are you?"

The child held up his hand, showing four fingers and a thumb to Billy Jo.

Mark had to clear his throat. "Billy Jo, Carmen called an ambulance. Is he hurt?"

Billy Jo looked over to him, fury flickering in the dampness in her eyes as she hugged the child close to her. "Can you get a blanket?" was all she said in response.

He looked back to his brother, who stared with horror. "Chris, can you ask Carmen to bring in a blanket? She has some in the trunk of her cruiser."

His brother only stared at the little kid, rattled. "Sure," he said, then dragged his gaze over to Mark as if he needed a minute to pull it together.

After Chris left, Mark turned back to his girl, who seemed to know just what to do. He loved Billy Jo more than anything, especially in this hell he was standing in.

"Can you bring him out?" he said.

She had her hand pressed to the side of the child's head. The boy was cocooned in her coat, hanging on to her. "I will. Just give us a minute, Mark."

He felt so damn helpless, and he backed out of the room without saying anything else. He heard the little boy say his name was Jay, and he paused and looked back, seeing him talking to Billy Jo, who was looking down at him and nodding. He knew Billy Jo so well and could tell she was really struggling. He made himself look away and started walking down the hall, where Carmen was leaning against the ladder, her back to him. Her shoulders were shaking, and he knew she was crying.

He cleared his throat roughly, maybe to save her dignity, and she straightened her back to him, sniffed loudly, and pulled her hands over her face, likely to wipe away the tears. He had to look away. *Keep it together, Friessen.*

"Carmen, did you call for the ambulance?" he said, then took in the ladder, realizing his brother must have gone out himself to the car.

She didn't turn around. "Yeah. Sorry, Chief, but they said the ambulance is stuck out on Lemur Flats and can't get out." She wiped her face again, sniffed, and turned around.

He was embarrassed for her, so he looked away and nodded. "Okay, we'll take him with us," he started. Then his cell phone rang, so he pulled it from his pocket, seeing Elisha's name on the screen. "It's Elisha," he said, then pressed the green answer icon and put the phone to his ear. "Where are you?"

He could hear Billy Jo behind him and glanced back to see her coaxing the child out of that boxlike room, then lifting him in her arms while wrapped in her coat.

"I'm on my way," Elisha said. "Just got a call from the lab. The ID came back on the prints of that woman. Her name is Ollie McCormick. She's from Bellingham, Washington, and she's got some priors for assault. I asked for the details and am waiting for a call back. You recognize her name, Chief?"

He was drawing a blank. "No, never heard of her."

"You think she's connected to the minister in any way?"

Mark lifted his gaze, taking in the low ceiling. "I don't know. Maybe. But two dead on the same night on my island? It's the kind of coincidence I don't believe in." He turned to see Billy Jo holding the child, whose innocent brown eyes should never have seen anything like this.

"I'll see you when you get here," he said, then hung up and turned back to Carmen. He relayed what Elisha had told him, then said, "You going to be okay?"

She glanced past him to Billy Jo, and he sensed that

she was pissed off, likely from him asking. "I'm fine, Chief."

"Good, because I need you and Elisha to take all this apart. Take pictures and bag everything. Billy Jo and I'll take this little boy to the hospital. And one more thing: You find out for me what the hell Kyle was doing down here."

Carmen stepped away from the ladder. He realized his brother was standing at the edge of the opening, holding a blanket.

"Here it is, Mark," Chris said.

He glanced to Billy Jo, who was holding the child, who was holding her. "I'll take him up," he said.

Billy Jo shook her head. "No, it's okay, Mark. I've got him."

## Chapter 10

Billy Jo was in the back of the Jeep, her arms shoved in Mark's coat because the little boy sitting beside her was wrapped in hers. Jay was five years old and terrified, yet he was surprisingly together for a kid they had found locked up. She had an idea of what he had gone through, but she didn't know how far she could push him to talk.

"You promise I won't be hurt. You won't take me back and lock me up?" Jay said.

He was so damn sweet. Chris, who was in the passenger seat, kept looking back at her and the little boy, whereas Mark was doing his best to drive in whiteout conditions on roads that were barely passable. He hadn't said one word since putting her in the back with the little boy, who was surprisingly small for his age.

"You will never go back there, I promise you," she said. "We're going to take you to the hospital right now and have a doctor make sure you're okay. Can you tell us how long you were down there?"

It was dark in the Jeep. From the smell, she thought

the little boy had been sitting in his own urine. The anger that continued to overwhelm her had her wishing the minister were still alive so she could kill him herself. She feared what he'd done to the boy.

"I don't know," Jay said. "A long time, really long. Ms. Billy Jo, do you save kids?"

She knew he was looking up at her, and it wasn't lost on her that Jay had never asked for his mother or father, his family. "I'm a social worker. I help little kids like you." She looked over to Chris, who was watching them.

"Billy Jo and my brother do rescue kids, Jay," Chris said. "They're the good guys."

Mark was pulling into the hospital, which she could just make out ahead, the tires on the Jeep slipping in the deep snow. Jay was looking at the big building, the lights, and she could feel him tense as he shook his head, still holding on to her.

"I don't want to go," he said.

Billy Jo unfastened her seatbelt as Mark opened his door and stepped out. She had heard the panic in Jay's voice. She unfastened his seatbelt too, and he reached for her. "I'm going inside with you," she said. "I promise it will be okay. No one is going to hurt you. This is a hospital with good people. They're going to help you and make sure you're not hurt." She tried to sound reassuring as she took in the dirt on his face. His dark hair was shoulder length, with a natural curl, and knotted.

"You promise you won't leave me?" he said. His arms were bare, and he was shaking as he held on to her. Mark moved the seat forward and stood outside, the Jeep still running.

Chris pushed open his door and stepped out. "Mark, I'll park your Jeep," was all he said.

Mark was waiting patiently, though Billy Jo knew he had to be cold. She slipped out, and his hand was right there to help her. Jay stood up in the back, and Chris waited off to the side as Mark reached in, holding his arms out to the little boy.

"It's okay, Jay," Billy Jo said. "I'm going to marry this guy."

Jay went to Mark, who lifted him out. He was still wrapped in her coat, but his bare feet were sticking out.

Billy Jo reached for Mark's arm as he started walking to the emergency room entrance. The doors slid open, and as they walked into all the light, she could really see how dirty Jay was. The emergency room was crowded, likely people trying to get out of the cold. The power was out, but not at the hospital, where the generators had kicked in.

Mark pulled out his badge and walked up to the nurse behind the desk. It was hopping busy, and she barely looked over, taking a chart. The phones were ringing.

"I'm Chief Friessen," he said. "We found this little boy, and he needs to see a doctor. Do you have a room available that's private?"

Maybe the nurse understood from his tone, as she immediately looked at him and then over to Billy Jo. She had dark hair and a round face. Billy Jo didn't remember having seen her before.

"Yeah, this way," she said.

Billy Jo followed Mark, who was still carrying the boy, to a curtained-off area. Mark sat Jay on the gurney.

"I'm Billy Jo McCabe, with social services," she said to the nurse. "Can I talk to you out here? Jay, I'll be right back. Mark is going to stay with you."

Billy Jo stepped out, and Mark reached for the curtain and pulled it closed. She turned to the nurse, who was only a few inches taller than her. "We found him locked up, trafficked, suffering the kind of abuse that should never happen to a child. Do you have a pediatric doctor on tonight?"

The nurse glanced to the curtain and back to her. "You suspect sexual abuse?"

She suspected a lot of things and didn't know how Jay was as okay as he was. "And then some. We found him hidden and locked up."

The nurse nodded and touched her arm. "Yeah, Doctor Kolter is on tonight. I'll page him. So you'll have an emergency placement for the boy?"

"I'll work something out," was all Billy Jo said.

As the nurse walked away, she slipped off Mark's bulky coat and made herself take one breath and another. She couldn't get her feet to move. Then she spotted Chris walking her way, brushing snow off his head. Behind her, in the curtained-off area, was the little boy whose story she was trying to get herself ready to hear. She really shouldn't be having this much trouble.

"You think he's going to be okay?" Chris stopped right in front of her.

Billy Jo ran her hand over Mark's coat and squeezed the heavy fabric before looking back up to him. The awkwardness lingered. "I hope so, but right now, I'm remembering the room where he was locked up. We don't know how long he was there or how many others were with him. Those clothes in the corner belonged to a little girl, yet we didn't find one. I don't have words right now. The little boy in there is looking to us to save him, but we don't know anything about him, or what he's been through, or what's been done to him."

Chris looked away. He wasn't made for this. She could see it from the way he pulled back. But then, she wondered how many were made for this. He nodded and gestured past her. "Tell Mark I'll be in the waiting area, and I'll call the house and let them know where we are."

Then he was walking away, and she realized he needed some distance. Could she blame him? Not really. Billy Jo made herself put one foot in front of the other and parted the curtain gently. Jay was sitting on the gurney still in her coat, looking right at her.

She forced a smile to her lips. "Chris is going to wait out there," she told Mark. "He's calling home and letting everyone know."

"Jay was just telling me he doesn't remember his mother," Mark said. "He said he was somewhere else before he came here, and there were three other kids he came with. A little girl named Pat was in his room with him. Jay, you said she was two?" Mark was looking at the little boy again, his hand on the gurney beside him.

Jay was looking up at Mark with the kind of hero worship she'd seen many times in the faces of children.

"And Ben and Alex," Mark continued. "You said they were eight and nine years old?"

Jay was nodding. "Alex was seven. Pat cried every night for her mom."

Billy Jo fisted her hands. Hearing this had that little voice in her head screaming, and she wanted to press her hands over her ears.

"You okay?" Mark said, touching her arm, and she nearly jumped. He pulled his hand away and gestured toward the boy. "Jay, you have to be hungry, thirsty? I can get you some juice, something to eat…"

Jay was playing with his fingers. He nodded. "Can I have apple juice?"

"And how about pizza, if I can find some?"

The little boy's eyes widened, and he nodded, excited for something so simple.

"Okay," Mark said. "I'm sure the cafeteria is open. I'll be right back."

Billy Jo wondered how Mark could be as okay as he was. She made herself paste a smile on her face as his gaze lingered on her for a second. Damn, she really loved him, but she couldn't say anything. He stepped around her but didn't touch her, and the curtain fluttered as it parted just a bit. Mark had stopped at the desk just as a doctor approached and was talking with him.

She made herself look back over to Jay and took in his round face.

"Ms. Billy Jo, can you find Pat? The man took her."

She put her hand on the gurney beside the little boy, who was so young. The image of him trapped in that room with a two-year-old was killing her. "We're going to look for her and find her. Do you remember who took her? Was it Kyle Drake, the old man in the house?"

Billy Jo helped kids, but this was different. Jay didn't look away from her at first, but then he did, looking past the curtain. He had started whining, low, freaked out, scared, and he reached for her.

"It's okay," she said. "What's wrong? I'm not going to let anyone hurt you." She pulled him closer.

He was looking out the curtain to where Mark was talking to the doctor. Kolter specialized in pediatrics.

She'd seen him a few times when she'd had to pull a kid from a home.

"That's just the doctor talking to Mark," she said. "Do you see someone? Do you recognize someone?"

The little boy was pointing now. "That's him."

"Who?" she said, her hands on Jay's arms. She bent down to him, and his tiny hand pointed out toward Mark, to the doctor. She looked at Kolter and then back at Jay, seeing the terror there. "Jay, look at me. The man talking to Mark, do you recognize him?"

The little boy nodded.

Billy Jo swallowed a thick lump. The heaviness in her chest was there again, and she turned back to watch the doctor. He had thinning dark hair and was of average height, round in the middle, in a dress shirt with a white coat pulled overtop.

"Jay, you need to tell me where you've seen him," she said, looking right at the little boy. She could feel him trembling.

"He took Pat," he said in a voice that was just above a whisper.

She wanted to say he was wrong. He had to be wrong. Mark was looking right at her, still talking to the doctor, and all she could think was no, this couldn't be true.

---

## Chapter 11

---

Billy Jo's face was pale, and from the way she set her hands on the boy's shoulders, Mark knew something was going on.

"Doctor Kolter, the lab is on the phone for you about the test results you were asking about," said a male nurse behind the busy desk, holding out the phone.

"Can you tell them I'll call them back?" Kolter said. He was looking right at Billy Jo and the boy.

Mark wanted to hurry the doctor in. He had met Kolter a few times, one of two pediatric doctors on the island, and the man knew about his upcoming wedding to Billy Jo. He felt the urgency, wanting to remind the nurse that the little boy he'd brought in had just lived through a horrific experience. A simmering cesspool had cracked open on his island and become something from his worst nightmares.

"Sorry, they said they're leaving," the nurse continued. "Do you want the results tonight?"

Someone else had walked over with another chart.

So much noise and so many people were chaos for an island hospital.

The doctor let out a sigh. "Mark, just give me a minute," he said. "But you and your fiancée don't need to stay. Thanks for bringing him in. I think the psychologist is still here, so I'll have her come down as well. We'll look after him and see he gets the help he needs tonight. Hey, Chad, can you call over to social services…?"

Mark already knew Billy Jo wouldn't be okay with any of that, considering Lisa Jenkins was way down on their list of social workers she'd want anywhere near Jay. "Thanks, Doc, but if it's all the same to you, I think we'll stick around," he said. "The wedding is kind of on hold with the storm, and I'm sure Billy Jo will want to make some calls about the boy."

Kolter shrugged. "Sure. Just give me a minute and then I'll have a look at him."

Then he reached for the phone, and Mark looked back to see Billy Jo lifting Jay off the gurney. He headed for the curtained-off area, and she gestured toward him sharply, eyes wide.

"What are you doing?" he said as he stepped in. Jay was holding on to Billy Jo as she lifted him.

"We're leaving," she said.

He wondered whether his eyes bugged out. "The doctor's right there and you want to leave?" He looked over at Jay and realized in that second that she didn't mean leaving the boy.

"Jay said he took Pat," she said.

He knew he was frowning as he turned and looked out, seeing the doctor on the phone, the nurses and other staff still behind the desk. "Who?"

Billy Jo's mouth was tight, and fear filled Jay's eyes

and face, the kind of petrification that had Mark wondering who it was he had seen.

"The doctor you were talking to," she said.

Mark just stared at her and was about to laugh when he realized she was serious. He gestured with his thumb. "You're talking about Doctor Kolter, the pediatric doctor? We know him." He wanted to add that there was no way.

"Mark, please. Jay said it's him. He's the one."

Mark dragged his gaze back to Jay. "You sure, Jay? That doctor standing there in the white coat with the phone?" He expected the little boy to say no, not him. But he could hear Jay's shallow breathing, and then he nodded slowly and leaned over as if he needed to whisper.

"The doctor came," Jay said. "He took Pat. It's him."

Mark's ears were ringing. This couldn't be true, but the fear in the boy's face told him it was. He looked over to Billy Jo. "Take him out to Chris and get in the Jeep."

She only nodded. Mark reached for his coat and stepped out of the curtained-off area just as the doctor hung up the phone. He walked right over to him.

"Doctor Kolter, can I have a word with you?"

The doctor glanced around him with his blue eyes and made a face, likely at Billy Jo walking out with the boy. "Where are they going?"

Mark glanced once to Billy Jo, who was carrying Jay past reception and over to the waiting area. He stepped over so the doctor had to turn his back to them. "Fresh air. Listen, can you tell me if you know the minister, Kyle Drake?"

The doctor smiled and shook his head. He made a

face again, and Mark had the feeling it was best to say as little as possible to this man, with the snowstorm and with Carmen and Elisha still at the minister's, combing the crime scene. He had to wonder how many others on the island were part of this. God damn, he knew there would be more.

"Kyle?" Kolter said. "Everyone knows Kyle. He's a staple of the island. I think he's married just about everyone, baptized all the babies born here, and preached every Sunday for more than thirty years. I don't understand why we're talking about Kyle, though —and, honestly, taking the boy out isn't ideal. I haven't released him, there's a snowstorm, and he's likely traumatized. I'll order a sedative for him and have him checked in and sent up to the pediatric floor. I'll keep an eye on him."

Mark pulled his arms across his chest. If he allowed that, would the boy disappear? "You know where we found him?"

The doctor appeared confused. "Actually, you didn't say, Mark. Why am I getting the feeling I'm being interrogated?"

He angled his head, wondering what he expected to see—nervousness, guilt. But instead he saw tired and pissed off. Maybe Jay was wrong. He hoped he was. "I'm not interrogating you. Just asking some questions, is all. We found the boy at Kyle's."

The doctor pulled a face and moved to step back. "At Kyle's? Well, where is Kyle? Why…? I don't understand." Either he really didn't know anything about what Kyle had been up to, or he was a damn good actor.

"Well, that's the thing, Doc. Kyle is dead. He was

stabbed. And while looking around, we found a trap door in the dining room that went down to a basement cellar, and you know what we found down there?"

The doctor's white face paled. "What! Are you saying Kyle is dead?"

Shock, surprise… Either Mark would be apologizing soon, or he wouldn't be.

"Unfortunately," he said. "You ever been out to Kyle's house?"

The doctor's entire expression was stony, and he seemed to need a minute to get his head around what Mark was saying. "You know what, Mark? I have no idea what you're alluding to, but I'm getting the very distinct feeling you're trying to point the finger at me. Do you think I killed Kyle? I barely knew him. And you can ask anyone here, but I was at the hospital all day. Don't be focusing any of this on me. I'm not a fool, Mark. I'm a doctor, a very busy one, and whatever this is, I'm not having it. I have no idea what Kyle was up to. I'll just chalk this up to pre-wedding nerves. The snow-storm is making everyone tense. It brings out the worst in people sometimes. Now, if you'll excuse me, I have patients to see." The doctor took a step around him and started walking the other way.

"Hey, Doc, you didn't ask what I found under the house or where we found the boy," Mark said.

The doctor still had his back to him. He turned his head without looking right at him. "You know what, Chief? If it's all the same to you, if you want to talk to me again, call my lawyer."

Then Doctor Kolter kept walking down the hall, leaving Mark with that feeling he got when he knew he was right. Damn, the knot was twisting in his stomach now, and all he could think was that three more kids were missing. Alex, Ben, and two-year-old Pat...

He shut his eyes for a second before glancing up the hall to where the doctor had disappeared, then to the door Billy Jo and Jay had already walked out through.

He thought of the woman in the church with his family's names on a list, Kyle Drake stabbed in his home, and the little boy who had been locked in a hole. In that second, a case that hadn't made any sense suddenly did.

---

Chapter 12

---

"Chris, let's go," Billy Jo said as she walked over to Mark's brother, who was by the vending machine, staring into it as if considering what to buy.

"You're done already? Where's Mark?" Chris frowned at her, noticing she was holding Jay.

Billy Jo put one foot in front of the other and glanced only once back to Chris. He was so different from Mark—quieter, she thought, but with the same tall, rugged build and likely just as stubborn. He fell in beside her.

"He's coming right behind us," she said, keeping her voice low, "but we have to go now. We'll explain it as soon as we get out of here."

They kept walking, one step and then another closer to the door. There was security, a desk at the door, a man she remembered seeing a few times, with a dark face and white dress shirt, the uniform.

He was looking up to her now, then stood behind the desk and said, "Excuse me, miss. Can I help you?"

Why was he standing? He was big, round in the middle, and he had started around the desk, glancing between her and Jay, who was gripping her shirt. Something in the way he was looking at her and Jay told her this could go sideways quickly.

"No, thank you," she said. "We're just leaving."

He was right in front of her now, holding his arm out to block her, but he glanced over to Chris, maybe thinking he was going to have some trouble. "I can't let you do that, folks." His other hand went to his belt.

"What do you mean you can't let us?" she said. "You can't stop us from leaving. I'm Billy Jo McCabe, from DCFS, and we're leaving right now."

"Seriously, you heard the lady. Move aside," Chris cut in, sounding unusually calm. She looked over to him.

The security guard shook his head. "I'm going to need to see some ID from you. Can't let you walk out into a snowstorm with a child looking like that." He gestured to Jay, and Billy Jo thought of her ID, which was tucked inside her bag, a logical place except for the fact that she'd left her bag at home.

Then the man looked past her. "Chief Friessen, could use some help over here," he said. "Caught these two sneaking out with a child. Not sure what's going on, but I remember he came in with you not that long ago."

Damn, he was loud. Billy Jo turned to see Mark striding her way, holding his coat, his gaze going right to her.

"Rashon, it's fine," he said. "They're with me—my fiancée, Billy Jo, and my brother Chris." Mark was right there now and pressed his hand to her back. Her heart was hammering as she glanced down to Jay, who was so quiet, looking to her to keep him safe. "You should put my coat on, Billy Jo…"

"Oh, so you're the social worker coming for the boy?" Rashon dragged his gaze from Mark to Billy Jo and back and frowned. "Betty said she had called DCFS, and a social worker was coming but wouldn't be taking him tonight. Was supposed to keep an eye out for her and take her in. What was her name?"

What was this man doing? He walked around the desk as if trying to get to the bottom of a mystery.

"I'm the head of DCFS on the island here, Rashon," Billy Jo said. "Don't worry. I'm handling everything." She leaned in, feeling how close Mark was to her.

"Then who is Lisa Jenkins?" Rashon said. "I wrote it down because Betty was clear that with the snowstorm out there, the child would be staying. I was to make sure the worker from social services was directed back to him. I have it right here. Hey, Betty," he called out, "can you explain to me why you gave me the wrong name from child protective services? I thought you said it was Lisa Jenkins."

Why was the security guard so stuck on the details? Billy Jo dragged her gaze to the door. Ten more steps and it would slide open. Then she looked up to Chris and wondered what was going through his head. She glanced down to Jay again, who was wide eyed. As small as he was, he was becoming heavy. She had to adjust him in her arms.

"Mark," was all she got out before he reached for Jay.

"Hey, come here, you." He handed her his coat as he took Jay. The boy was still wrapped in her coat, his face smudged and dirty, peeking out as the nurse walked over. Betty was the head nurse, someone Billy Jo had talked to previously.

"What's going on?" she said, letting her gaze linger on Billy Jo and then Chris and Mark. Her smile brightened her light round face.

"It's the little boy," Rashon said. "You said social services had to be called. I remember you said the boy had just come in, but the chief and his fiancée, who is a social worker, say they're leaving and taking him with them. Yet I don't see the paperwork here. You said the boy wouldn't be leaving tonight, with the snowstorm and all."

She looked up to Mark again because this was ludicrous. Since when had security ever stepped in like this? They sat at a desk, answered questions, gave directions, and read the newspaper.

"Billy Jo, hi," Betty said. "I thought you were off on leave. You're getting married! Congratulations, by the way. I talked to Lisa Jenkins. She's filling in for you. I guess maybe you got your wires crossed or something. I didn't know you were called too. I just spoke with Lisa. She was on her way down."

What the hell did Betty mean by "down"?

"You mean driving here?" Billy Jo said.

The nurse was shaking her head. "No, she's here already. She was with some kids she brought in this morning and went back upstairs again with the administration." Betty gestured behind them and said, "Did Doctor Kolter already see this little guy?"

Fifty questions were exactly what Billy Jo didn't

want. All of this was making her really uneasy. It was as if a spotlight were shining on them.

"Doctor Kolter left," Mark started.

Betty smiled and waved to someone behind them, then said, "Left? He can't leave. There are patients waiting to see him. Why didn't someone tell me he was leaving?" She frowned.

Billy Jo wondered what was coming next.

Betty glanced around her and waved. "Hey there, Lisa. I guess you can sort this out between you all while I find out who's on call now. Oh, and, Chief, if you don't mind waiting, I'll have to grab the paperwork before you leave."

Billy Jo turned to Lisa and slid her hand on Mark's back, holding his coat in her other arm. Lisa wore a short dress, ankle boots, a silky scarf, and glasses, and her hair was pulled back—not exactly dressed for the weather. What was it about this very young woman that she didn't like?

"Lisa, there's nothing for you to do here," Billy Jo said. "I've got this."

"With all due respect, Billy Jo, I'm on call. In fact, until you're back, all calls are supposed to come to me. Is this the boy I was called about? Because I'll take it from here." She was standing so close, reaching up to touch Jay, who whined. Mark stepped back with him.

"Are you kidding me, Lisa?" Billy Jo said. "Don't touch him." She stepped in front of Mark, forcing Lisa to step back, and felt her hands fisting.

"Oh, excuse me, Chief?" said Betty, hurrying their way again. Why the hell was she insisting on being so damn efficient tonight?

"What the fuck…" Chris said under his breath, then

leaned down and said in a low voice to Billy Jo, "You want to fill me in on what's going on here?"

She only shook her head and glanced once to him.

Betty was holding a chart. "Chief, wait. I think there's some confusion about Doctor Kolter. No one knows anything about him leaving. I just sent him a page."

How could this be happening? Billy Jo touched Mark's arm, aware Rashon was still standing behind them, and Lisa was still there too, like a pit bull, ready to challenge her. Even Nurse Betty was suddenly going to be a problem.

"Doctor Kolter isn't coming near this child," Billy Jo snapped, jamming a hand into her hair.

Betty blanched and seemed to pull back. "What are you talking about? He's a pediatrician. Why wouldn't you want him seeing this boy? What's going on here?"

Lisa was showing too much interest, too.

"Well, okay, let's talk about that," Mark said. "You've worked with Dr. Kolter for how long? What can you tell me about him? How long has he worked here? You seen him bring in a little girl recently, a little girl by the name of Pat, about two years old?"

Betty frowned and angled her head. "Dr. Kolter has been here…I don't know, three years. He's fantastic, a good doctor. You're not talking about his niece, are you?"

Billy Jo's heart was thumping, and she leaned in. "His niece? When was this?" she said, taking in the confusion in Betty's expression.

"Yesterday, I think. Why are you asking all these questions about Dr. Kolter? I don't understand what this all has to do with the little boy here."

Mark turned to Billy Jo. "Here, take him," he said. "Chris, stay with her."

Damn it! The way he said it, she knew he was up to something.

"Mark, what are you doing?" she said.

"Just give me a minute."

"What's going on here?" said another doctor walking over. "Hi, Chief, is there a problem here?"

The man was overly interested, older, blue eyed, with a thick head of hair, a mix of dark and white. Billy Jo had seen him a few times, and apparently, he knew Mark. In the crowded waiting room, more than a few people were looking their way. They were attracting way too much attention.

"Doctor Leonard," Betty said, "it's about the boy the chief brought in with the social worker. He's been *abused*..." She lowered her voice. "I'm not sure what's going on, but the chief is asking questions about Dr. Kolter."

The doctor was so close that he pulled at the edge of her coat. He smiled at Jay. "You brought this little guy in? And you found him where? Hey there, I'm Dr. Leonard," he said.

Billy Jo didn't know where to look. She was fisting her hands, very aware that Lisa was still there.

"You know, why don't I have a look at this little guy, and then we can have a talk about what's going on?" Leonard sounded so calm, and he gestured back into the emergency room.

Mark looked down to Jay.

Maybe it was her own fear Billy Jo was having to deal with, as she found herself saying, "Mark, I would rather go."

He didn't pull his gaze away. She knew the doctor was watching her, and Lisa too. "I know," he said. "But let's go back in. We'll stay with him, and then I'll find out what the hell is going on here."

Chapter 13

"Where did you find him, again?" asked Doctor Jon Leonard, who Billy Jo realized was the head of the ER.

"A crime scene," Mark said. "Kept in a bunker, locked, and there were other children."

She stood right beside him, her hand on the gurney where Jay was sitting in an old shirt. He really needed a bath.

The doctor pressed his stethoscope to Jay's back and listened. "Take another breath for me, Jay," he said, then looped the stethoscope around his neck. Betty stepped in and had to slide around Chris and Lisa, who just wouldn't go away.

"Thanks, Betty," Leonard said. "I want a full workup on Jay, and I want to get him a gown. How about this, folks? I know you're all concerned, but it's getting a little crowded in here. I assure you he's fine…"

"Not happening," Billy Jo cut in. "If you want to examine Jay, I'm not leaving."

"The doctor's right, Billy Jo," Lisa said. "Since

you're not officially on call and I am, I'll stay with him. I'll find an emergency placement for him." She already had her cell phone out. Something about this young woman was frustrating the shit out of Billy Jo.

She reached over and pressed a hand to Lisa's phone. "Can I talk to you a second?

"Okay, folks, how about one of you stays?" Leonard interrupted.

Billy Jo glanced back to Jay, who was taking all of this in, his expression still spooked.

"And I'd like to have a word with you, Chief," the doctor continued, "and whoever the social worker of record is."

Billy Jo fisted her hands. "That's me," she said, as she had realized Lisa wasn't going to let it go.

"I'll stay," Chris said.

Mark pressed his hand on her lower back and stepped out of the curtained-off area, leaving Chris and Nurse Betty. The doctor stopped just off to the side, close to the desk.

"Look," he said. "Just a quick examination of the boy tells me he's been malnourished, and what I'm seeing is evidence of abuse. He's how old?"

Lisa had pulled her arms over her chest stubbornly. "Five, he said," she replied. "Can you tell if he's…you know, been abused in that way?"

Billy Jo had to roll her shoulders, because she suspected as much but didn't want her head going there.

"With the evidence I'm seeing, it's likely," Leonard said. "I'm going to call for a psych to come down, as well. I normally don't do this, but we could get him checked into the pediatric ward tonight until social services figures out what to do with him."

"I'll take him home tonight," Billy Jo blurted out, then looked over to Mark. "Mark…"

He reached over and slid his hand over her back. "Yes, we'll take him tonight."

"No, hang on a second here," Lisa said. "I'm in charge. We have many qualified families he can be placed with. With all due respect, Billy Jo, there's a protocol that has to be followed, and I'm not signing off on a boy going home with you." She was outright challenging her. "So no, Dr. Leonard, you finish your evaluation of the boy, and I'll make some calls. And if I can't find a bed for him tonight, please book him into the pediatric department if possible."

Billy Jo reached over and gripped Lisa's arm.

"Hey!" she squealed.

"Excuse us, please," Billy Jo bit out through gritted teeth. She glanced back to see a hint of amusement in Mark's expression as she pulled Lisa out with her.

"Let go of me right now!" Lisa said as Billy Jo pulled her around the corner. She was digging her heels in, staring at Billy Jo with fury from behind dark-rimmed glasses. "How dare you grab me like that? I think you bruised me."

"I did not. Would you knock it off? What is wrong with you? Why are you even here? In case you didn't notice, there's a snowstorm out there, and Jay is not a ticked box in a file. He's a little boy we pulled out of something truly horrific…" She leaned in. Her voice was low, and maybe it was her tone, spitting mad, warning Lisa not to fuck with her, that had Lisa stepping back and bumping into the wall.

Billy Jo had to remind herself to cool it. Her heart thumped, and the heavy breath she dragged in did little to calm her. She fought the urge to snarl as she stepped back, realizing she had overstepped. "And challenging me? Just where do you get off doing that?"

"I have a job to do," Lisa said, "and with all due respect, Billy Jo, don't put your hands on me again." She actually pulled her arm away.

"I'm sorry if I upset you," Billy Jo said, and Lisa lifted her chin, her mouth set tight. "Just what are you doing here, anyway?"

"I'm following up with psychiatry on the Clark girl, the oldest one. I brought her in earlier today. She's in bad shape, and I'm considering recommending to the judge that the parents not get the children back."

Billy Jo lifted her hands to her temples and pressed, reminding herself to breathe. "Ah, yes, the two girls you took from Nathan and Grace. Mellie is the eldest one's name. You thought pulling her from her family would solve what, exactly? You do realize she has Rett syndrome?"

Lisa just shrugged and shook her head, dismissive.

Billy Jo angled her head. "That's in addition to autism and PDD, as various doctors have told the Clarks. In other words, she's severely disabled. So explain to me why you felt the need to take her from parents who were doing their best. Let me guess: The hospital locked her upstairs, maybe medicated her because she was freaking out, or maybe they tied her to the bed to keep her from shoving things in her mouth or playing with her diaper, something Nathan and Grace struggle with every day. Tell me, why were you on their doorstep in the first place? Did a call or complaint come in?"

Lisa was defensive, not wanting to be questioned, at

least not by her. Did she understand what she'd done? "It was a wellness check, Billy Jo. That's what we do as social workers." She leaned in, and Billy Jo had to remind herself not to put her hands on her despite the fact that Lisa would likely cause a lot of destruction and broken families.

"Why were you doing a wellness check on the Clarks?" She knew the file had been in the drawer of families she was trying to help get funding.

"It's a policy I have, especially in a new place. There was a file—"

"In my desk drawer," Billy Jo said, cutting her off.

"That doesn't matter, and it's a good thing I looked, too, because I could not believe the condition of the premises. There were locks on the doors, and the girl was naked. I have good reason to believe they may have been locking the girls in the rooms. There was feces on the wall and the floor. The conditions weren't habitable. They're better off with the state." It was so matter of fact, the way she said it.

"You truly believe those kids are better off with people who don't even know how to care for them? Do you even understand what Rett syndrome is, or PDD, or autism? Do you understand the social anxiety, the degree of nonverbal communication, or the fits and outbursts Mellie has? They lock the doors to the other rooms because she will smear feces everywhere. She isn't toilet trained—and it isn't for lack of trying. She screams at times and is inconsolable. They've been to umpteen doctors, which is the reason for the multiple diagnoses, because none of them can agree. They haven't been able to get medical help for her because they can't afford it. So you know why I had that file in my drawer?"

Lisa said nothing. She wasn't sure she was getting through to her.

"Because I was searching for resources for them. There's funding if you really dig, and I'm trying to help them, not destroy the family. You think you're helping Mellie by having her locked in a psych ward, maybe pumped full of drugs? Then what? You think there's a magic cure for that child?" She shook her head. "There are millions like her in this world, and there's no help unless the parents have resources. The psychiatrist here will release her, and you'll stick her in some foster home, but do you think those foster parents will have any clue what to do? They won't, because the kids are a paycheck to them.

"This is what will happen: She'll be locked in a room, but because her foster parents will be approved by the DCFS, that will be okay. They will take the extra money that comes with a child with a mental deficit, and when they've collected enough, they will call you to pick her up, and then you'll toss her in some institution, all the while telling some judge how unfit her parents are!"

She was fisting her hands again. "Lisa, go home. You've done enough damage for one day. Don't add that little boy in there, who's been through absolute hell, to the list of children whose best interests you're not thinking about."

For a moment, Billy Jo thought Lisa was going to argue with her. But she spotted Mark walking her way. It was just the way he moved, everything about him. He had a way of making things right even in what seemed like a very dark time.

"Everything okay here?" he said, looking at Lisa. Then he dragged his amazing blue eyes over to Billy Jo.

"I'll be going, then," Lisa said. "You be sure to file the paperwork and send it to Grant. I will not have this coming back on me."

Billy Jo figured that was the best she was going to get. "Drive safe," she said. "The roads are bad and visibility is zero."

Lisa went to step around Billy Jo, then stopped and stiffened, pressing her lips together and looking right at her. "I made a judgement call," she said. "I'm sure there've been times you've done the same thing."

Billy Jo let her gaze soften a bit, then gave her head a shake. "No. You see, Lisa, taking a child should never be done without carefully considering everything—the situation, the family, what's really going on, and maybe, just maybe, you should see if there's something you can help with. Because I know firsthand that pulling a child from his or her home should only ever be done if it's in that child's best interest. More importantly, you need to know that where you're putting that child isn't worse than what you've pulled her from."

Lisa let her gaze linger, then turned and walked away without saying one more word. Billy Jo felt Mark's hand on her shoulder.

"Well done," he said as he slid his arm around her, then pressed a kiss to the top of her head.

She leaned into him. This was just another thing about him that was perfect, she thought as she looked up into all that tall handsomeness. "I'm sorry I didn't ask you first about taking Jay home."

He pressed a kiss to her lips, soft, quick, and pulled back. "It's okay. You just beat me to it."

## Chapter 14

As the wind and the storm echoed through the house, a feeling of the power and fury of Mother Nature went through Mark—along with a feeling that the worst was yet to come.

Jay was on the sofa in the living room. The candles in the kitchen cut through the darkness, and Billy Jo had just covered the boy with one of the quilts from their room. Chris was having a heart to heart with J.D., Danny, and Evie, filling them in on the scene Mark still needed to go back to. He was more relieved than he could have explained that Chris was the one telling the family about the horrors they had seen.

"So what are you planning on doing with the boy?"

Mark hadn't heard his dad walk up. Jed rested his hand on the corner of the wall, and his mom was there too. Rose, meanwhile, was carrying another blanket and pillow into the living room, where Billy Jo was saying something to Jay.

"Haven't thought that far past tonight," Mark said. "I still have a crime scene at the church, which will have to wait until daylight, and one at the minister's. I think we can safely say the wedding is off. Maybe someone was looking after us. I can't believe Kyle Drake would have married us…"

He realized Chase was there now too. Billy Jo's father pulled his arms across his chest, glancing over to her and Rose.

"Then there's the dead woman in the church," he continued, "who I guarantee is tied to the minister. Don't know all of her story. Did she kill him?" He lifted his hands in the air. He was missing something, a piece of the puzzle he still needed to put together.

"You're carrying a lot on your shoulders," Diana said. "Billy Jo said Jay never asked for his mother. Do you know where he came from? Mark, seriously, I don't even know what to say about this island. I thought it was a sleepy, quiet place."

He glanced over to Danny, Evie, and J.D. From the little candlelight they had, he could make out their expressions and knew they were having some trouble getting their heads around what Chris was telling them.

"I don't think he knows who his mother is," Mark said. "It sounds like the only life he's known is this. I just don't understand how someone does this to a child, an infant. It's sick. And no, Mom, I never realized what secrets exist here. But it's not just here, is it? It's everywhere, just hidden better. Ever since arriving here, I've realized crimes against children exceed anything I could have imagined. I don't think anyone has any idea how many kids go missing every year. The trafficking… What happens to them, and who's really behind it? I didn't know. Once your eyes are opened, you see child trafficking operates on a scale that seems almost untouchable. I thought it was off the island."

No one said anything, which was good, considering he didn't want to talk about it anymore.

"Look, I have to go," he said. "Carmen and Elisha are still at the minister's house, going through everything. I'm hoping they'll find something that ties him to the woman at the church and maybe gives me an idea why she had a kill list and how she knew about all of you."

"You just be careful out there," Chase said. "I can come with you."

Mark pushed away from the wall. "No, I'll be fine. You're better off here, keeping an eye out," he said. Then he headed over to Billy Jo and Rose. Billy Jo must have seen him, as she stood up, pressed her finger to her lips, and started toward him.

"Is he asleep?" He kept his voice low, sliding his hand over her arm.

"Not quite. He's fighting it, but he's exhausted. You're going back, aren't you?"

He touched her cheek. "Yeah, I have to. There's a lot to go through, and who else is out there? The storm hasn't let up. I'm sorry…"

She wrapped her hand around his wrist and held on. "Don't apologize for anything. None of this is your fault. I'll get my coat." She let out a sigh, and he let his hand fall away.

"Why?"

She looked up to him, and even in the candlelight, he saw the stubbornness. "I'm going with you."

He shook his head. "You should stay here with Jay. I

don't know how long I'm going to be or what else I'm going to find."

She reached over and touched his arm again. "That's why I'm going, Mark. Jay will be fine here with our families, and I can be more help to you. Don't argue. You know you won't win."

Then she walked around him, and Rose, who he hadn't realized was listening, strode over to him. He wasn't sure what to make of her odd expression and the way she shook her head.

"We got Jay," she said. "You just look after my daughter. I know you know this, but I'm going to say it anyway: She's strong minded, strong willed, and once she has her mind made up, you cannot change it. You know what she survived as a kid. She would understand better than anyone what Jay has been through, but she still has wounds that haven't healed."

He realized Rose often kept her worries for Billy Jo to herself.

"Yeah, I know," he said. "Thanks."

Then he strode to the front door, where Billy Jo already had her coat on and was sitting on the bench, pulling on her boots. There was his dad, too, with a shotgun and his coat and boots on.

"Dad, what are you doing?"

Billy Jo didn't look up to him. There was something determined about the two of them. He realized he was out of arguments.

"Going with you," Jed said. "Chris, Danny, and Chase are here to keep an eye out. You think I'm letting you both walk out there in this with no one watching your back? I may not be the police chief, but I'm still your father."

The way his dad spoke was quiet but so familiar. The man had taught him who he was, and Mark realized he wasn't going to win this round. Billy Jo handed him his hat and gloves and stood in the little light from the battery-operated lantern.

"Well, let's go then," Mark said. His dad pulled open the door, and Mark took a flashlight from Billy Jo and reached down for her hand. "Stay close. Don't let go of me."

She didn't argue.

He let go of her hand and stepped outside, very aware of his sidearm. The wind whistled, and the force of the snow coming down was blinding. He could barely see anything but felt Billy Jo's hand on his arm as she reached for him. The snow was deep, and he could just make out where his Jeep was, the snow already covering it.

He glanced back once to see his dad, another light behind him, and then bumped into the Jeep. When he pulled the door open, the inside light popped on, and he moved the seat forward so Billy Jo could climb into the back. His dad had the passenger door open as Mark started the engine.

"I'll clear the snow off," Jed said, resting the shotgun on the floor in the back and reaching for the windshield brush.

Mark lifted his gaze to the rear-view mirror, seeing his girl, whom he wanted to marry more than anything. "I'll make it up to you, you know. The wedding."

She was looking right at him. Then the passenger door opened, and his dad climbed in before she could answer.

"Let's go," Jed said. "There's a lot of snow out there. Pretty risky, Mark."

He put the jeep in gear and realized how crazy all this was. "It's my job, Dad," he replied. He wondered what his dad would say to that.

Jed gestured toward him. "You always did things your own way no matter what anyone said."

Mark had his wipers going full speed. "You complaining? Pretty sure you're the one who taught me to be who I am."

His dad grunted. "I tell myself that every day as I watch you and your brothers, all of you. Just wait until you have kids. You know what the hardest thing is?"

"I don't know, Dad. What?"

"You have to let your kids make their own mistakes and fight that urge to step in and fix it for them. That's the hardest part. Maybe that's why I'm so damn proud of you. You're a good man, Mark—but your mother won't be as understanding."

Jed tapped his arm, and Mark gave the Jeep some gas and gripped the wheel as he plowed through the snow.

—————————

## Chapter 15

—————————

As he took in the dead minister and climbed down into the hidden cellar, Mark wondered whether other cops had such dark nights of the soul. Carmen and Elisha appeared neck deep in evidence, papers everywhere, cupboards wide open to reveal binders with names and files. The cellar felt like a dungeon under the house of a man who was supposed to have been of God.

"You find anything?" Billy Jo was standing off to the side, quiet and looking around, taking everything in again. He didn't have a clue what she was thinking, and he wondered how much of what she was seeing stirred up everything in her that she had never made peace with. He was well aware of the demons she carried and the fear she struggled to overcome just to be with him.

"Pictures, records, notes going back decades," Carmen said. "But what I can't figure out is why there are records here from child protective services."

Mark frowned, and behind him, Jed muttered, "What the hell…?"

He glanced back to his dad, not recognizing the look

on his face now. "Dad, this is a crime scene, so don't touch anything," he said.

Jed narrowed his gaze. "Where did you find the boy?" he asked gruffly.

"At the end," he said. "Dad, this is what I do, but you may not want to look. It's in my head, what happens to these kids, but you don't want it in yours."

He wasn't sure his dad agreed.

"I'll show you," Billy Jo told Jed, and in that moment, Mark knew she understood him in a way no one ever could. He turned back to Carmen, who was holding out a piece of paper.

"You want to explain why child protection is sending copies to a private company?" she said, looking over to him. Elisha was still sorting through papers and files.

"What are you talking about?" he said, taking the page she handed him, a record of a child taken in Yakima. Carmen pointed to the bottom of the page, which indicated it was a fax copy of a report to the Hanover Foundation. He shook his head as Carmen handed him several more pages.

"At the bottom of each page," she said, "right on the reports. These are from the DCFS across Washington, and we found some from Oregon, Nevada…"

"Billy Jo," he called out before Carmen could finish. He stepped back to see his girl standing in the doorway of the cell where they'd found Jay. Both his dad and Billy Jo turned toward him as he said, "Can you explain what this is?"

He held the paper out and jabbed his finger at the fine print at the bottom. She flicked her blue eyes up to him, and he had to fight the need to protect her. Did she have any idea how hard it was for him to just step aside, knowing he couldn't shelter her from this?

"What is it?" she said.

"Look at the bottom. What is the Hanover Foundation?"

She made a face and looked down to the paper, taking it from him.

"Chief," Elisha said over her shoulder, flicking open a binder, "this foundation is a private company, from the looks of it. The fax number is here. Why is a government agency sending detailed copies of records of children who were taken into care?" She shook her head. "Look at this. With all of these, someone has circled the age and sex and made note of the skin color of the child."

Mark didn't know where to look. He thought of the minister, a man who had been in the community for decades, and reached for the binder. Billy Jo was stiff, still looking at the paper, and she hadn't said anything. Jed was right there too, saying nothing.

"Babe, I know this is hard," Mark said, "but you know anything about this? Since when does a private organization get access to these records?"

"They shouldn't be sending anything to a private company," she said. "I remember this case. How many are here? I can tell you I never faxed this to anyone. There should be a copy in my files and a copy to the state. Can you tell who is sending them?"

"Yeah, right here," Elisha said, and Billy Jo walked over to the counter.

Mark nodded to Carmen and moved over toward the ladder, looking up. "Tell me you have something here that points to Kyle Drake being part of this foundation," he said.

Carmen handed more papers to him. "Yeah, looks that way. You're going to want to see this. I found this in the fax machine, sent today. See the names on there? They're the two little kids from this morning, Grace and Nathan's girls. It came from this office."

He took in the official report, the copy, and then looked back to Carmen. "Sent from here? So Kyle Drake is basically a predator running an underground ring with access to CPS records and he's, what, filling orders? Good God, I think I'm going to be sick. Lisa Jenkins faxed this." He handed back the paper. "You find anything down here that ties to the good Doctor Kolter? I mean, this is real sick. A minister and a pediatrician are people you're supposed to be able to trust."

Carmen only nodded. Mark glanced back to see Billy Jo and Elisha talking and going through papers, binders, whereas his dad was looking at a chain on the wall. The little kid's clothes had already been bagged up as evidence. Mark swore he'd never get anything about this out of his head.

How many tears, how many screams had come from the children Drake had been keeping down there? He wanted nothing more than to climb out and drive away and wish he had never seen any of this. But he knew that wasn't realistic, and he thought of what a betrayal it would be to the little boy they'd found.

"Mark," Carmen said, "with all due respect, I can see in your face how hard this is for you. Sometimes it's okay to say you can't do this. I remember when I lost my kid, how it happened. When social workers come in and you disagree with their tactics or butt heads with them, it works against you. I don't know what these kids' stories are, the homes they came from, but I do know that oftentimes, social workers have no feeling or compassion. They destroy far too many families, and the rights of parents like Grace and Nathan are hardly respected. What I saw this morning, and so did you, is a father who wouldn't kiss Lisa Jenkins's butt or thank her for coming, and now the identities of their kids have been given to a monster."

He didn't know what to say. "I'm not weak, Carmen. I'm human, and maybe I wish I didn't have to see this, but I will not look away. I get what you're saying, but Billy Jo isn't like that. She'd never do this. She became a social worker to stop this and to be a voice for these kids."

Carmen glanced once over her shoulder and back to him. "I know that, and I know there are more Billy Jos out there, but it seems the bad guys are starting to outnumber the good. And they're getting sneaky, Mark. What the hell are we fighting here? How many more are doing this on the island? Where else is this happening? This is a lot of kids, and how many of them were even reported missing?"

He knew what she was saying. Maybe that was another reason he was so unsettled.

"I hate to say this," she continued, "but I think you should call Tolly Shephard. He knew Kyle. Hell, most of the island did—well, at least the people who run things. They've had him over for dinner at their tables with their children…"

Then everything went dark.

He looked up. Someone had a flashlight on. "Damn! The generator. I should have checked to see the fuel level. I'll go now. How many flashlights do we have?" he said, feeling creeped out down there in the dark.

"Take mine," Carmen said. "The generator is in the shed right out the back door. Not sure how much gas is left in the can."

"You want me to go with you, son?" Another flashlight popped on.

Mark shook his head as he took in the ladder. "No, I'll only be a minute," he said, then started up one step and another into the darkness. He hefted himself over the edge, his light flickering on the body of the minister, when he heard the distinct click of a safety behind him.

"Very slowly, Chief." The voice was female. "I want you to close up the door to the cellar. Easy now. I don't want to have to shoot you…"

"Who are you?"

There was the sound of a round being loaded in the chamber of a shotgun. It was distinct.

"Mark, what's going on up there?" Carmen yelled up, and he heard her foot on the ladder.

"Close it now, Chief, or I shoot the first person who comes up here."

He didn't think. He reached down and lifted the trap door just as he saw Carmen coming up the ladder, and he closed it before she could reach the top.

"Now slide the lock, Chief." The woman sounded young.

He realized he'd dropped his flashlight. "I need light," he said. "I'm just going to reach for my flashlight." His heart was thudding.

"Just the flashlight, and do it slow."

"Mark, what the hell?" Carmen yelled from below. "Open up!"

He could hear the banging as he reached for the flashlight and shone it over the door. He set his hand on the bolt, then flicked the light over, seeing two legs in boots.

A gun fired to his side, and wood splintered and hit his face. He heard a scream below.

"I said lock it! Next time, the bullet goes right through the floor."

He slid the bolt and felt something wet on his face. Blood, likely. "Who are you? What do you want?" He was holding the flashlight and could still the hear yelling from below—his dad, Billy Jo, Carmen. But he wasn't listening.

He flicked the flashlight up as he stood slowly, and he realized he was staring down the barrel of a shotgun held by a young woman he didn't think could be more than seventeen or eighteen. She wore a heavy coat and a hat over her blond hair, which was thick and curly. The way she was looking at him, he knew she'd pull that trigger and shoot him without blinking an eye. Her hand trembled.

"I want my kid, Chief."

"You know who I am?"

She angled her head. "I know exactly who you are, Chief Mark Friessen."

He knew angry, and this young woman was just that. "You kill Kyle?" he asked her.

She made a face. "You mean did I stab that sick motherfucker when he didn't tell me where my daughter was?" She let out a rude noise. It wasn't a laugh.

"You don't look old enough to have a kid," he said. "How old are you?" He could see the shotgun was heavy for her. Everything about this was dangerous.

"Old enough to have a kid but not to vote or drink. Back up, Chief, or I will shoot you, you sick fuck."

He lifted one hand and took a step back, pulling in a breath. "Kyle took your daughter? I'm not your enemy. Why don't you tell me your name and put the gun down? I'm here to help. I will find your child."

He took a step, but she lifted the shotgun, and he could see she wasn't going to hear him.

"Now, why would I believe you, Chief, when you looked away as this man used his church to do the most vile, disgusting things? How many kids did you look away from? He wouldn't tell me where Pat was, but I know what he does down there. I know he sells kids. He moves them. Someone puts in an order. The blond ones always get more money, and the younger they are, girls or boys…"

"You have the wrong man," he said. "I have never looked away from a crime. You want me to help you, then put the gun down. I can't help you this way. You said you have a daughter, Pat?"

Her lips were tight, and she gave a sharp nod.

"You know anything about the woman in the church?" he said. "Ollie…"

"McCormick. Yeah, I know her. That bitch is the one who found me when I tried to get away. She took Pat. She was always there, every time I was sold and moved."

His heart was thudding again. "She had a list in her hand…"

"You talk a lot. You think I don't know you're part of it? She told me the chief on the island looked the other way. This island is where it all happens. The social worker here gave her the names of the kids. So I asked around and made the list. Not hard on an island of people who love to tell everyone about everyone's families. But they don't give a damn about you when you're taken by child protective services, and next you're on a boat or in a trailer with a bunch of other kids, sold. You have any idea what happens to kids like me? I was eight when I was first taken. I enjoyed killing her. You almost seem as if you care, but I'm not that stupid anymore, Chief…"

"Drop the shotgun, little lady."

He heard the click of a gun and the voice of the old chief. Tolly was pointing his gun right at her from the doorway to the kitchen, so close, yet Mark had never heard him come in.

Everything happened so fast. She yelled and went to turn, and Mark lunged forward. His hand hit the barrel and shoved it up just as the gun went off.

## Chapter 16

Mark's knees gave out, and he hit the ground. His ears were ringing, a pressure wave having smacked the side of his head. He squeezed his eyes shut and pressed his hands to his ears, feeling thudding from below the floor—yelling, pounding, footsteps. There was another gunshot. Where was his flashlight? He felt around for it on his hands and knees. Was he shot?

He grabbed the flashlight as he pulled in a breath that echoed long and loud in his ears. He stumbled to his feet, taking in the shotgun on the floor, and shone the light toward the back door, where Tolly Shephard stood in the doorway. Mark had his gun in his other hand now, and he staggered a bit, bumping the wall as he widened his jaw to try to relieve the pressure. He slapped his ear, still holding the flashlight.

"Chief, where is she?" he said, bumping the wall again.

"She ran out into the storm," Tolly said. "Crazy…"

The wind was howling. Mark tossed his head again, hearing yelling and pounding on the trap door.

"You hurt?" Tolly said. "You got blood on your face."

Mark reached up and wiped the back of his hand over his face, feeling the wetness.

"Mark, what's going on?" Carmen yelled from below. "Open the door!"

"I'm fine," he said. "Shotgun went off by my head. My ears are still ringing…" He hurried across the tiny old kitchen back to the dining room and knelt down to slide the bolt and lift the door.

"What the hell were you doing, Mark?" Billy Jo said as she climbed up after Carmen. "You locked it? Who was shooting?" She shone another flashlight, as they were all in the dark.

"When I climbed up, there was a girl here with a shotgun, just a kid, a teenager," he said. "Wait. Tolly, why are you here?"

Jed had climbed up last.

Carmen had joined the old chief. "I called him," she said so matter of factly, then turned back to Mark. "You didn't check the generator?"

He shook his head. "No. She was waiting for me. Don't know who she is, but she killed Kyle and the woman in the church. It's about a kid. She seemed to think I was part of it."

Billy Jo was in front of him. "Mark, are you shot?" She touched his face. "You're bleeding." She gripped his chin a little too hard.

"Hey, go easy," he said. "It's just a ricochet, likely a piece of the floor. She wanted her kid, Pat…"

Billy Jo wiped his face with her hand.

"No," he continued. "Look, I'll go after her. She ran out into the storm."

"She had a shotgun on you and was going to kill you, Mark," Tolly said.

Mark was trying to get his head around the fact that the old chief was suddenly there. The timing was unusual. "Did you shoot at her?"

Tolly shook his head. "I yelled at her to stop and shot a warning in the air, but damn, she was fast. She kept running."

Mark realized he was still holding his gun. He shoved it in the holster and pulled his coat down over it. He looked over to his dad and Elisha, then back to the old chief, remembering the girl's hatred as she had stared back at him and what she'd said about the chief looking the other way.

"I'm going after her," he said.

Billy Jo slid her hand over his cheek. "No, you can't. It's dark. You'll be wandering around blind out there. I'm all for going after someone, a kid like that..." She let out a heavy sigh and pulled her hand away, angry. "You're going anyway, aren't you?"

He handed her his flashlight. "Have to," he said, then pulled his hat from his pocket and over his head.

His dad gripped his shoulder, stepping closer. "Son, you get lost out there, you could freeze to death." As Mark pulled his hood up, his dad handed him his gloves. "Take these. Your tracks are going to be covered in five minutes..."

He knew what his dad was saying, and he nodded. "You'd do exactly the same as me," he said, then reached for the flashlight. He glanced to Tolly and Carmen before turning back to Billy Jo and saying, "Stay here."

She slid her hands over his cheeks and pulled him

close, then pressed a kiss to his lips. He pulled away and started walking but stopped in front of the old chief.

"When I get back," he said, "you and I need to have a talk."

Then he shone the light out the back door, seeing the whiteout. He let the door close behind him as he stepped out into the blinding snow, squinting as the storm raged and the flakes pelted his face. He lifted his arm and shone the flashlight at the ground, looking for any sign of tracks, and knew how right his dad was. He took one step and another, the snow getting deeper, up to his knees now, before he spotted what looked like tracks.

He kept the light on it. His ears were ringing from the shotgun blast or the whistling of the wind, or likely both. He kept going, one foot in front of the other, toward a spot where it looked like she had fallen. Damn, it was blacker than anything out, and his light shone only a foot in front of him, barely.

He kept moving until the ground beneath him suddenly declined, and he slipped and went down, rolling. He put his foot out, scrambling to get his footing, when he saw something, someone, and heard a shriek.

"Stop!" he yelled into the wind, grabbing her coat as he dug his foot in and managed to stop where the ground flattened out. God damn, it was her! "Hey, stop it! I'm not going to hurt you." He didn't know how he did it, but he managed to get her facedown on the ground, his knee in her back, and he pulled her arm back.

She screamed, "Get off me, you motherfucker! I'll kill you! Let me go!" She was feisty and fighting, and she swung out and hit his chin with her free hand.

"Stop!" he yelled. "I told you I'm not going to hurt you. I told you I would help you find your kid, but stop, already! You ran out into the middle of a storm. You'll freeze to death out here." He dropped his flashlight and pulled her other arm up, feeling the tiny wrist. This girl would go down swinging.

"Why would you care?"

"Because I'm not who you think I am. I would never look away from a crime, never let a kid be hurt. I only stumbled upon that cellar tonight, and I found a boy down there. Jay! Do you know Jay? He said there was a little girl with him, Pat, and she was taken." He felt her stop fighting.

"You know where Pat is?" In her voice was a keening just below the surface. He could hear her pain, her anger.

"I'm looking for her," he said. "If I let go of you, will you stop fighting me? We need to go back. Can you walk, or are you going to run again?"

She tossed her head side to side. "You lying to me?"

His flashlight was right there in the snow. He trusted nothing about her, but he leaned down closer, seeing her face in the snow. Her hat was gone. She had to be cold. "I'm not lying to you. What's your name?"

"Trix," she said, lying still as if the fight was out of her, but he was smart enough to know it could be a ruse.

"Trix, why would you think I would in any way be a part of this? I have a family, I'm getting married to a great girl, and I would never hurt a kid." He lifted his hand from her shoulder and then reached for his flashlight before he stood up, letting go of her wrist. "Don't run," he said, then reached out. "Here, come on."

She didn't take his hand, just rolled to the side and

stood up, brushing the snow off. She was small. He waited for her to bolt, but instead she said, "Kyle always bragged that the chief watched his back, and Ollie said one of the cops here on the island oversaw the shipments and made sure there were never any problems. You telling me you're not involved?"

That knot in his stomach came back out of nowhere. "I'm not involved. I've been chief on this island for a few months and had lived here for less than a year. You didn't hear my name from Ollie or Kyle." He didn't know what she was going to do, but he was prepared to grab her.

"They didn't give a name, but I asked around, and everyone said Mark Friessen was the chief. If you're lying to me, I'll kill you and everyone in your family."

The way she said it, he believed her. So he reached for her arm, shone the light ahead to the hill he'd fallen down, and said, "Let's go."

_______________

## Chapter 17

_______________

Billy Jo took in the snow Mark had tracked into the station. The lights were on from the generator, and Lacy was just coming out of the back room. She really did resemble Gail in so many ways.

Mark said something to the girl, Trix, and bars clanged as he put her in a cell, and then he walked back out with the cuffs and heavy blue coat she had been wearing. He tossed both on the desk and then shrugged out of his own coat, which he draped over the chair. The blood on his cheek had dried, and she could see in the light that the cut would likely leave a scar.

"Lacy, I didn't expect you to still be here," he said.

"Only have a cold house waiting for me, and I'm not chancing a drive in my Tracker. I've been in the ditch before. So I'm bunking down in a cell back there. Guess I have some company tonight."

Mark didn't say anything. Billy Jo could distinguish his many moods, and he'd been pushed to the edge and back tonight. She didn't know what to say to settle him down, or maybe it was her she needed to settle. She had never expected to love this man as much as she did.

She heard the door and glanced over her shoulder to see Jed carrying both shotguns, Mark's and the girl's.

"Where do you want these, son?" he said.

Mark let out a heavy sigh and walked past her, touching her shoulder. He took a shotgun and looked down the barrel, performing all the checks, the sequence to unload a gun and make sure it was safe.

"Here's the shells." Jed pulled them from his pocket.

Mark walked away to the back with both guns, and she knew he was securing them. It was something she watched him do all the time when he was carrying. He frequently ran through the safety checks on his gun at home before he locked it in the gun safe.

She felt a hand on her shoulder and took in Jed, whom Mark resembled in so many ways.

"You doing okay, there?" he said. He was quieter than Mark.

"Fine. It's been a long night. I should be tired, but I don't think I could close my eyes if I wanted to."

Jed Friessen didn't have Mark's brilliant blue eyes. His were the color of whiskey, and the lines around his eyes and mouth were more vivid. He gently squeezed her shoulder and then let his hand fall away. He was such a kind man, everything about him. Mark's family really did have each other's backs.

"I never imagined I would walk into that kind of place, that horror show," he said. "I know things like that happen, but seeing it…" He let out a heavy sigh. "I'm having some trouble understanding how a human being could do that to a child."

She wondered if Mark knew how lucky he was to

have a mother and father who loved him and his brothers as much as they did, who would protect their kids with their own lives. "That's the thing," she said. "Predators may look human, but they're monsters, and they are real. They look human and walk among us…"

"But he was a minister, a man of God."

She realized he really was having trouble understanding. "The perfect cover. I mean, who would question a priest, a minister? No one looks twice at people who do those jobs, social workers, cops, teachers, doctors… Nothing is off the table, and hardly anyone ever questions it."

She heard Mark walk out of the back room and wondered when she'd become so in tune to him. "Mark, what about that girl back there, Trix? Are you going to talk to her?"

He let out a heavy sigh and ran his hand over the back of his head, his neck. The edge of the cut on his cheek had a hint of purple, and she wondered if it hurt. He didn't have time to even think about it and would brush her off if she tried to clean it. He just wasn't the type to be fussed over.

"Yeah, I do need to talk to her," he said, "but she said nothing to me the entire way back. I wanted to have a word with Tolly, too. When did he leave, and why?" He frowned.

Billy Jo pulled her zipper down. "I don't know, Mark. He and Carmen went outside and started up the generator. It was out of gas, I guess. I think they were talking, and then he just left. Thought he was going to look for you, but Carmen said he had something to take care of. I didn't think anything of it. I was worried about you out there. You have no idea how relieved I was that you made it back."

He said nothing, but she knew he understood even though it was damn near impossible for her to say, "I love you." His cell phone dinged, and he pulled it from his pocket to read a message. "Carmen's car is stuck," he said. "She's coming back to the station in Elisha's four by four. They have Dr. Kolter's address. I'll leave you my Jeep, Dad, but I need to go to the doctor's house. If he took Pat, if what Jay said is true…" He let out a breath, and she could see the toll this was taking. He looked tired.

"I think I should talk to Trix," she said.

He angled his head and shook it, his expression turning obstinate. "No."

"Mark, just hear me out. She's not going to talk to you. I understand what she's been through. If anything, I think I may be able to get through to her. I saw the way she looked at you when you cuffed her at Kyle's. The hate she had, staring at Kyle's body… Then there's the kill list. If she did it, she isn't going to be suddenly willing to talk to you. I understand that kind of hate and anger. I know when she's going to bullshit me and go mute. You said someone told her you were part of this. I don't think you have the whole story, and that worries me."

He groaned and shook his head. "Fine!" he snapped, throwing a hand in the air. Then he pulled in a breath. He really was on edge. "Go talk to her, but if she asks for a lawyer…"

She slipped off her coat and glanced over to Jed, unsure what to make of the way he was watching her and Mark.

He pulled his arms across his chest. "You really are good for him."

She hadn't expected that. She walked over to the small fridge below the coffeepot and pulled it open, knowing Lacy always kept it stocked with soda. She reached for a ginger ale, then spotted a bag of cookies beside the coffeepot and reached in to take two. Mark and his dad were talking now, and Lacy was sitting in her chair, saying nothing, just watching and listening. Maybe she understood, as she gave Billy Jo a nod.

Billy Jo walked into the back cells, to the one on the end, seeing a girl with a thick mop of blond curls, wearing a dark blue sweater, sitting on a cot behind bars. "Hey, I brought you some cookies and a soda." She held the can through the bars and took in the frown on the girl's face. She put her other hand through with the cookies.

"You trying to buy me?" Trix said. "That's how it starts, you know, offering some freebie, a treat, an ice cream, a cookie."

She knew what she was talking about, and she knew what she was doing. "I'm well aware how a pedophile operates. I can see you've once been vulnerable, but now you're deeply scarred. You probably didn't even realize how easy it was to share your vulnerabilities through casual conversations. Or were you just taken? Mark said you were eight."

She still hadn't moved. Billy Jo squatted down and set the can on the floor just inside the bars, the two cookies on top of it. Trix's gaze tracked her motions.

"Why do you want to know?" she said. "I was a kid. You're trying to be nice to me to get me to agree to something. Then someone will come through that door and unlock the cell, and I'll once again be owned by someone."

This wasn't going to be easy. Trix was shaking but trying to hide it.

"Is that how it happened to you?" Billy Jo said. She recognized the tightness around the girl's mouth, the same she remembered from when she was young and angry. "Do you have family, someone we can call to let them know you're okay?"

Trix was looking right at her as she slid off the cot and reached for the cookies and soda. Then she went back to sit on the cot. Nothing. Silence.

"I'm getting married tomorrow," Billy Jo said. "Or I was, to that guy out there, Mark, the chief. But you already know who he is, or at least our names. You killed the minister? I guess maybe I should thank you, considering I now know what he did to kids, what he was doing. It would have tainted something beautiful. I was with Mark earlier. It's been a really long night. They found the cellar, and we found a little boy down there, the only one."

Trix took a bite of the cookie and popped the can of soda to take a swallow. "Where is he? Who did you give him to?"

Billy Jo gripped one of the steel bars. "We took him home because we don't know where he'll be safe. He's with my parents and Mark's family. They're keeping him safe. He talked about a little girl in that box where we found him. He said her name was Pat and she was two. You said you have a little girl. Is that her?" She had all her attention now. The recognition was there in her eyes, her face, the way emotion pulled across her brow.

"You know where my daughter is?" Trix snarled.

"Where?" She dropped the soda, and it spilled over the concrete. She tossed the cookies across the cell with anger. Billy Jo could see how fucked up this kid was.

"Mark has an idea," she said. "He's heading out now to find her. If she's on the island, he'll turn over every rock until he finds her."

Trix stood there in the cell, her hands fisted. "You're lying."

She ran to the bars, and Billy Jo stepped back because she knew the girl would have reached her and likely strangled her.

"No, I'm not. I'm not asking you to trust me, but Mark isn't going to hurt you or Pat. And he had no idea that the minister was trafficking kids. He'll shut it down, but he needs your help to do it. I need your help. Who told you Mark was responsible, that he looked the other way? He couldn't have known. He's been on the island less than a year, a little longer than me. From what I know about this island and its secrets, it seems we've only just scratched the surface."

Trix was gripping the bars of the cell. Then she pushed away, walked over to the soda can, and kicked it against the wall. She yelled, and it sounded like a roar. Bill Jo could see and hear how this girl had been destroyed from the inside out. Would she ever be okay?

"You think a cop here was helping?" she said. "It wasn't Mark."

Trix pulled her arms across her chest, and she had no idea if she was getting through to her.

"The woman in the church, how did you know her?" Billy Jo said. "Was she a friend?"

"She was no friend. She was my handler. She took Pat from me, but I got away. I knew what they'd do to her. They said she wasn't mine to keep, that they owned her because they owned me and could do anything with her. They could sell her. It's modern-day slavery."

Billy Jo felt as if two roads were converging. "Never really ended, did it?" she said. "Slavery. The most powerful out there, they want what they want. I grew up in foster care, and I know how fucked up the system is. I may not have been sold like you, but it wasn't that far off. I was rescued by my dad and my mom now, who got me out and adopted me. But I can see you weren't as lucky. It would help Mark to know who on the island was helping Kyle. You sure it was a cop? Because when he finds Pat, he can do only so much to keep her safe if another person is hiding in plain sight. They could come right in and take her and no one would question it."

Billy Jo wondered if this was all she was going to get. She'd hoped she would be able to reason with her, but Trix was likely too far gone. She pushed away from the wall and took in the mess in the cell before she started to walk away.

"Wait…!" Trix called out, hurrying again to the bars and gripping them.

Billy Jo turned back to her.

"Ollie said the chief on the island was the watcher, keeping an eye out, looking the other way. Told him when it was time to move the kids, when a shipment came in, always underground, always by boat. You say it's not Mark, so who else knows how to make reports about missing kids go away? Who else could make sure no one suspected the old minister of being the biggest trafficker of kids? He lined up buyers and took a cut, making sure no one came looking for any of us. He had an inside man who had access to a cop's database. You hear things. I heard things. When I strangled the life out of Ollie in the church with my bare hands, I knew the chief would be coming and would find her…"

"So you put a kill list in her hand?"

She smiled. "Every predator who bought me, male or female, liked to brag about what they were going to do to me, to others."

Billy Jo stared at her. "But you were going after the wrong cop. You never saw the chief."

The girl looked away and stepped back from the bars again. Was she getting through to her? Trix only shook her head, then looked over to her with pure emotion. "No, I only heard about the woman who worked for him."

Her ears were ringing as she stepped toward the cell. "Woman? What woman?"

Trix made a face. "His deputy…"

"What's her name?" Billy Jo said, unsure what to make of what was staring back at her.

Trix shrugged. "Only heard it once. Zarko."

---

## Chapter 18

---

Mark hated not being in control, sitting in the back seat of a four by four driven by his deputy, while Carmen was in the passenger seat. He could just make out a big house, two stories, with a car covered in snow parked out front.

"Carmen," Elisha said, "you sure you don't want me to go back to the minister's and secure the evidence? I can load it in my SUV and take it in as soon as we're done here."

Carmen shook her head. "No, I've got it."

"You put the files in your trunk?" Elisha asked. Mark knew the sheriff's cruiser Carmen had driven was now stuck in the snow.

"Locked in the lockbox," Carmen said. "I'll go back for the rest and get a tow and a plow to get my car out after we finish here. You sure this is where Dr. Kolter lives?"

Mark was listening to the back and forth. His phone dinged, and he pulled it from his pocket to see a message from Billy Jo: *Call me.*

He put his phone back in his pocket as Elisha stopped and put her four by four in park beside the snow-covered car.

"This is the doctor's house," Carmen said, "but we have no warrant, so how are we playing this, Chief?" She looked back to him, and he knew how sideways this could go.

"A seriously sick doctor on this island possibly has a two-year-old girl in his possession. He's likely bought her. I have to allow my head to go to that dark, ugly place of what he could be doing to her. Sorry, but there are lines you don't cross: kids and animals. To be clear, I'm going to do what I need to do to save this kid from a horrible fate. I'll ask for forgiveness later. I just pray I'm wrong." He yanked open the back door.

"And what if she's not here, Chief?" Carmen said. "You go through that door, and if he didn't take the kid, your career is over." In the light that had popped on inside the vehicle, her dark eyes reached out to him with a warning.

His phone dinged again, and he reached inside his pocket and pressed the button on the side to silence it. "Not now, Billy Jo," he said under his breath. "If she's in there and I wait, that's not something I want to take to my maker. I can't stand by because of a technicality and let some sick fuck hurt a kid. Being fired and losing my badge is something I can live with, but crimes against a child on my watch? I can't."

He stepped out into the howling wind and darkness. Elisha was in front of him, shutting her door. "You want to hang back?" he said. "Because I don't want what I do here coming down on you. Right now, you only drove. I'm willing to accept the consequences of my actions."

"Chief, I've got your back," she said. "I hear you, and there's no way I'm walking away. It's a little girl. If I lose my badge, I lose it, but at least I'll be able to look myself in the eye."

Mark reached into his coat and pulled out his small flashlight. He walked around his new deputy and took in Carmen, who was also walking around the front of the vehicle. Mark put his hand on the hood of the snow-covered car. Not ice cold, but not warm either. He walked up to the door, his flashlight on, taking in the deadbolt, and he hesitated only a second before pulling his sidearm and lifting his leg to kick the door by the lock. It burst open.

"Dr. Kolter, show yourself!" he yelled. "This is Chief Friessen." His flashlight illuminated the massive entrance, the walls covered with artwork. He gestured toward the living room. "Carmen, right," he said in a low voice, then gestured to the kitchen and said, "Elisha, left."

Mark took the stairs, listening as he made his way up. He thought he heard something, keeping his back against the wall. "Dr. Kolter, this is Chief Friessen! We know you have the girl, Pat."

He heard a whine and something else. God damn, it was the sound of a kid. His breath fogged, and he flicked off the safety as he made it to the top of the stairs and listened. Right or left?

"We have you surrounded," he continued. "You're not going anywhere. You let her go now. Come out here."

He heard a cry, he thought. It was faint, but he knew it was coming from the end of the hall. One more step, then another. The door was closed. He put his hand on the knob, gave a silent prayer he'd find the kid untouched, and shoved the door open, his gun and flashlight out, his finger ready to slip over the trigger.

His light flickered on feet, a chair. The doctor was sitting there.

"Get your hands right up, Dr. Kolter, or I swear I will shoot you!"

He didn't move. Mark's flashlight shone across the man slumped over, his arm over the side of the chair, a pistol dangling from his hand, touching the floor. He took in the blood on the side of his head, the glossed-over eyes. He shoved his flashlight between his teeth and reached out to feel his neck for a pulse. Nothing.

Mark flicked his safety back on and took in a cell phone on the floor. He reached for it as he holstered his gun.

"Chief, nothing here!" Elisha called out.

"Up here," he replied. He bent down, moved the pistol away, and reached for the dead man's hand to press his thumb to the phone. Then he tried his index finger, and the phone unlocked. He was staring at a message on the screen: *They're coming for you.*

"Chief, holy shit, is he dead?" Elisha said.

Mark glanced over his shoulder to the light his deputy was shining. He heard footsteps on the stairs, and there was Carmen too. "Yeah, he shot himself. Looks like he was warned we were coming." He held up the phone and shone his flashlight over both Carmen and Elisha.

When his phone buzzed again from his pocket, he didn't reach for it. Of course, it was Billy Jo. He was still staring at the text message that had warned the doctor. "The thing is, who knew we were coming here?"

He pressed the call icon with his thumb and heard another cell phone ringing immediately. He was looking right at Carmen and Elisha as he tossed the cell phone on the bed beside him, and he reached for his gun, feeling the gut punch of betrayal.

"Aren't you going to answer it?" he said.

There was something about the way she looked over to him, holding her gun.

"Put the gun down, Elisha," he said.

She lifted her gun, but another went off, and she screamed. Her gun was on the ground now, and she was holding her bleeding hand.

Carmen had shot her. She had her on the ground. "I should have known," she snarled.

Mark was still holding his gun as Carmen kicked Elisha's service pistol away. He heard a whimpering again. Elisha screamed as Carmen cuffed her injured hand.

Mark walked over to the closed door. He reached down for the knob and turned it, shining his light in, holding his gun. Sitting on the floor of the bathroom was a little blond child wearing a dirty white T-shirt. He shoved his gun in his holster.

"Hey there, are you Pat?" he said in a soft voice and crouched down to her. She had blue eyes. Her face was tearstained, and she nodded. He held his arms out to her. "Well, hi, Pat. I've been looking for you. I'm Mark, a police officer, and I'm going to get you out of here."

She reached her tiny hand over, and he lifted her up, then reached for a towel on the rack and pulled it around her, holding her close as he said, "Everything is going to be okay now."

$$\text{———————————}$$

# Chapter 19

"It's starting to ease up out there," Jed said, standing by the window. "Is Mark still not picking up?"

The darkness was just giving way to the dawn as another call to Mark went to voicemail.

"No," she said, feeling the bite as she spat it out furiously. She couldn't be nice. She was so damn helpless and worried. "I don't know why he's not answering."

She gripped the back of Lacy's empty chair with one hand, hearing her over at the coffee maker, pouring water. The aroma of freshly ground coffee lingered. Billy Jo was so past tired, but she knew she'd never be able to sleep.

"Why won't he pick up?" she said. "He goes on and on about me not letting him in and not returning his calls when I'm busy or working, as if he's keeping track of me during the day, and now he can't pick up the damn phone! Damn, how could I not have seen it with Carmen? She's so private and elusive and screwed up, and…"

Jed said nothing, leaning against the window, looking

out. Then he glanced over to her. She didn't know what he was thinking after her rant. He was careful with his words, she realized, considering everything before he opened his mouth. "Mark's back," he said.

Relief hit first, followed by a wave of anger. She heard footsteps, and the door opened, and there was Mark, holding a child wrapped in his coat. The girl had curly blond hair and blue eyes, clinging to Mark. Billy Jo had to fight her first instinct to run to him.

Carmen followed next, bringing in a cuffed Elisha. What the fuck? A bloody cloth was wrapped around one of her hands.

"Mark, what's going on?" Billy Jo said. "I called you. Why is Elisha cuffed?" She gestured toward them as Mark walked over to her.

"Damn, be careful. That hurts," Elisha complained.

Billy Jo found herself looking over to Jed, who headed over to her and Mark, evidently as confused as she was.

"This is Pat," Mark said. "Found her in Kolter's bathroom. He'd put a bullet through his head." Mark sat Pat on the desk, and his coat fell away to reveal a blue towel wrapped around her. Her feet were bare and red, and she was so tiny. She had to be cold. "Can you get a blanket for her? Pat, this is Billy Jo. She's going to help."

Billy Jo glanced over to see Lacy already walking out of the back, holding a folded gray blanket. Carmen dragged and pulled Elisha over to her desk. Blood dripped on the floor.

"Take these cuffs off me," Elisha said. "This is inhumane, cruel…"

"Shut up," was all Carmen said to her, leaning in

and pressing a hand to her shoulder to make her sit in the wooden chair with a thunk.

"I need a doctor," Elisha demanded. "Take me to the hospital. I've lost a lot of blood. My fingers…"

Billy Jo didn't know where to look. She touched Mark's back, his face covered in dried blood. The little girl, Pat, was looking up to him with the same hero worship Jay had, and she reached for him, terrified.

"Mark, what is going on?" she said again. "I called you, texted you. Carmen…" She gestured over to her, her voice just above a whisper.

He shook his head. "It wasn't Carmen. It was Elisha. She texted the doctor to warn him. I saw your text. Sorry, but when your call came, I couldn't answer." He took the blanket from Lacy with thanks and then shook it out and wrapped it around the little girl. "How is that, Pat? Are you warm now?"

The little girl nodded. She had her fingers by her mouth. "Yeah," she said, then stood and reached for Mark again. She was scared of Billy Jo, Jed, Lacy, all the strangers standing around her.

The cell rattled from the back room.

"Pat!" Trix called. Obviously, she had heard them. "Let me see my daughter! Pat!"

"Mama," Pat said in a quiet voice.

Mark picked her up again. "You see this lady here? I'm going to give you to Billy Jo."

She shook her head. "Uh-uh."

"You should take her back," Billy Jo said, but the way Mark was looking at her, he likely didn't agree.

"Mark, I've got her," Lacy said. "I'll take her to the back." She walked around Billy Jo. "Hey there, Pat. I'm

Lacy. You come with me, and we're going to see your mama."

She didn't know how Lacy did it, but Pat went into her arms, blanket and all, and then she was walking into the back. She could hear the rattling of the cell door, and then she thought she heard crying from Trix. She couldn't make out what she was saying.

Mark ran his hand over his face, rattled. She touched his arm, and he reached for her and pulled her close, kissing the top of her head and holding her. Damn, he felt good, and he was squeezing her so hard.

"You scared me," she said.

"Sorry." He kissed the top of her head again. Then he stepped back, but his hand lingered on her. The lights flickered, and she could just make out the sputter of the generator before it stopped. The sun was coming up, though, so it didn't leave them in the dark.

"Mark, there's no gas left," Lacy said, poking her head out, still holding Pat. "I used the last of it hours ago."

He lifted his hand to show he had heard, but it was just one more thing being piled on him. When he stepped back, she again realized the weight of everything he was carrying.

"Mark, when I spoke to Trix, she said it was Carmen," Billy Jo said, keeping her voice low. "She had her name, Zarko. That was what she heard, that there was a cop watching things. Elisha hasn't been here that long…"

He ran his hand over her shoulder again. She didn't know why he wasn't all over this. "It's not that simple, babe. There's way more going on. I don't have time to explain it." He looked over to Carmen. "You get in her phone yet?" he said to her, walking around Billy Jo.

She wanted to yell at him, but instead she found herself looking over to his dad, who was watching his son with curiosity.

Carmen was holding a cell phone, and Elisha was sitting on the edge of the wooden chair. She had to be hurting, as she rocked back and forth. Mark was standing above her, looking down.

"You want to do this the easy way or the hard way?" he said. "Give us the passcode. We'll get in there one way or the other."

Carmen was punching in numbers, and she held up the phone. "Come on, Elisha. Tell me, and then I'll take you to see a doctor." She sounded so cold.

Elisha shook her head. "Lawyer." She looked up at Mark.

"You want a lawyer?" he said. "It's going to be a while. Storm, no power, and pretty sure the phones are down."

What was Mark doing?

He pressed his hands to the desk, leaning down so close to her. "How long have you been part of this? Who brought you here? Who else is involved?"

She still didn't answer.

Billy Jo stared at Carmen, who was holding the phone, glancing between Mark and Elisha.

"I can't," Elisha finally said, shaking her head.

"You can't?" Carmen said. "You were awfully helpful tonight. With all that evidence in the cellar, it was as if you knew where to look. You know, I almost trusted you—almost. But there was something there, and there was no way I was letting you take what we found. If any of those files, those binders, those notes disappeared… You kept asking to take it. You heard the chief, Elisha. Start talking. The minister has been keeping kids in that bunker, selling them. Who else is part of it? How many kids have passed through here? Who bought them, and what was your role?"

Billy Jo couldn't look away. She didn't understand why Mark had ignored her about what Trix had said.

"I said I want a lawyer. You heard me." Her voice was gravelly.

Mark was still staring down at her. "You can have a lawyer, but you won't be getting any deal. Trafficking, crimes against children—you'll never see the light of day. You'll go to hell and burn for eternity. Who else is involved?" He slammed his hand on the desk so hard the sound ricocheted through the precinct, and Billy Jo jumped as a file spilled to the floor. She'd never in her life seen Mark lose it like this. He pulled his holstered gun and held it at Elisha's head.

"Mark, what the hell are you doing?" Jed yelled.

Carmen had jumped back, and her chair tipped over and hit the floor. Yet Elisha seemed so calm with the gun to her head. She shut her eyes, her mouth tight.

"Dad, back off," Mark said. "I'm counting to three, and then I'll start shooting you. There're a lot of places I can shoot and not kill you, but it will hurt a hell of a lot. I'll start with your knee." He lowered the gun, pointing it at her knee.

Billy Jo had to remind herself Mark wouldn't do this. He was bluffing. But she wasn't so sure. Jed put his hand over her shoulder. She couldn't look away.

Elisha shook her head. "I can't! They'll kill me," she yelled up at him.

Billy Jo hadn't expected that, but Mark didn't back down.

"You're out of options," he said. "I will keep putting bullets in you until you talk. Who is involved on my island? How many kids are you moving through here? How long has this been going on?" He moved his gun away and pulled back the slide, putting a round in the chamber.

Billy Jo was terrified of how far he'd go.

"There are six rounds in the magazine," he said. "That's a lot of bullets, a lot of hurt. I will make you suffer, and then I'll get a doctor to patch you up, and I'll put you in a cell, and I'll put word out that you're talking. You think they'll ask first to make sure it's true. They won't care. They'll come for you. Your only chance to save yourself is to give up names. You want to live?" He had yelled it at her.

Elisha was fighting against giving in. "Fuck you," she spat out. "Fuck you, Mark Friessen! I want protection. You guarantee me that, and that I will walk, and I'll give you all the names, every fucking name—every ward councilor, every judge, an ex-president, an attorney general, a military general, a senator's wife, Hollywood royalty, bankers, Wall Street executives, people who run the CIA and FBI, even a foreign leader. This isn't just here. It happens all over the world. I'll give it all to you, but only after I get a guarantee."

Mark flicked on his safety and emptied the round from the gun before holstering it. Then he reached down for the bullet on the floor and sat it on the desk. He grabbed Elisha's arm. "Get up." He wasn't gentle.

"What are you doing? Where are you taking me?"

He said nothing, just turned her around, slid the key

in the cuffs, and undid one from the hand wrapped in the bloody cloth. He re-cuffed her hands in front of her, then strode over to his coat and pulled it on.

"Where are you going?" Billy Jo said.

Mark didn't look at her. Fury simmered in him beneath the surface, and he let out a hard breath. She knew he was likely beyond words. She pressed the flat of her hand to his chest before he could zip his coat, and he flicked his gaze down.

"I can see you're angry," she said.

He pressed his hand over hers and let out a sigh. "Sorry. I love you. I've gotta go."

She'd never seen him like this.

He stepped back and looked past her again. "Carmen, take her to the hospital, stay with her, and then bring her back and park her in a cell. Then I want you to get all that evidence. Get it back here." He reached down and slid his hand under Billy Jo's chin. "There's one more person I need to find. Go home. You'll have to take Pat…" He shut his eyes and gave his head a shake.

"Son, you need to give yourself a minute," Jed said. He had been far too quiet, but she could hear the warning.

Mark zipped up his coat, then turned to his dad. Something passed between them, and Mark nodded but said nothing to him. "Lacy!" he called out, and she appeared from the back, holding Pat. "I need you to drive my dad and Billy Jo home, Pat can go with them."

"What about Trix?" Lacy said.

Mark reached for his cuffs on the desk and tucked them into the pouch on his belt. Then he pulled his coat down over them, shaking his head. He reached for the keys to his Jeep, which he had tossed on the desk. "She stays. She killed two people. I need you to come back when you're done. I know you've been here all night and are tired…"

"It's fine, Chief," Lacy said. "We're all tired."

When Mark started to the door, Billy Jo followed him, setting her hand on his arm as he pulled it open. The snow had stopped, and the sun was coming up.

"Mark, what the hell is going on?" she said. "None of this makes any sense. Elisha? How?"

He ran his hand over her hair. "It's not as it seems. Nothing is here. This island seems like a sleepy, quiet, idyllic place to live, to raise a family. Maybe that's why it's the perfect place to do the kind of thing no one would suspect. There are so many private docks here, and how many waterfront estates? And there's just me to watch over it all. I'll talk to you at home. Please take Pat. You'll have to find a place for her."

"Don't worry," she said. "But you didn't tell me where you're going."

He didn't look away. Something flickered in those blue eyes, and she saw he wouldn't hesitate to cross a line. He was so right and yet so wrong. She wasn't sure what he'd do, how far he'd go. She'd never seen him this far off the rails.

"You ever wonder how an underground child trafficking ring ended up on this island?"

She didn't know how to answer that. "No, but I'm wondering if you have some idea. You sure Carmen isn't involved?"

He said nothing at first, and his breath fogged. "She isn't, but I know who's neck deep in it. Look, I've got to go." He went to step out. The snow was deep, and his Jeep was covered.

"Wait, Mark, who?" she called out after him.

He pulled open the door of his Jeep, and she felt the knot in her stomach tighten as he just stared back at her.

"Tolly Shephard," she breathed out.

He angled his head, his expression inscrutable. "I'll see you at home. Try to get some sleep," he said. Then he climbed in the Jeep and started it, and Billy Jo walked back into the station.

Lacy was holding Pat, talking to Jed, and they both looked over to her as she walked in. Carmen was with Elisha. All she could think was that today would have been her wedding day.

"You okay, Billy Jo?" Jed had walked over to her, holding keys.

"I'm fine."

He nodded and patted her shoulder. "No, you're not. None of us are. I'll go warm up Lacy's Tracker and clear it off. You just keep doing what you're doing with Mark. He's a good man. I'm proud of him. With what he's had to deal with here, you're his rock."

He gave her shoulder another squeeze and walked out of the station, and she looked down at the ring on her finger, gave it a twist, and then fisted her hands.

It was the other way around. Mark was her rock.

------------------------------

## Chapter 20

------------------------------

Mark watched as the snowplow made its way down the main road. The hydro crew were already working on one of the many downed lines as he put his cell phone to his ear and listened to the ring. He knew Tolly had picked up the phone. He said nothing, but Mark could hear him breathing. "Where are you right now?"

"Cleaning up," Tolly said.

The knot in Mark's stomach pulled tight. "Where? I'm not asking again."

"I think you know where, Mark." He slurred his words, and Mark wondered whether he was drinking. "Kyle Drake lived in a rectory built by the church twenty-six years ago."

He heard rustling in the background. "So you're at Kyle's? Stop playing games with me, Tolly."

"I'll see you when you get here, Mark." Then he hung up.

Mark gave his Jeep more gas and made his way around the snowplow, seeing the church now in the light of day, snow covering it. Damn, he was supposed to be there today with his family, marrying his girl. Not a chance he'd ever consider marrying her there now.

He skidded and made his way through the thick snow. The tracks from just hours ago were gone. He spotted the house, the Shephards' pickup, and Carmen's cruiser, all covered in snow. He pulled up behind the cruiser, the trunk of which had been pried open, and parked his Jeep, turned off the engine, and climbed out.

He gave his door a shove and looked around, seeing no one and nothing. He lifted the busted lock on the trunk and took in the open lock box, empty, the evidence gone.

"Fuck!" He fisted his hands, feeling the cold, dragging his gaze back to the house, and he trudged through the deep snow past the truck and to the back door. Only hours ago, he'd brought Trix back with him.

He pulled open the back door, listening to the generator still running, and stepped inside. In the living room, the body was covered with a blanket, and light spilled up from the bunker tunneled under the house. He pulled his coat up over his holstered gun, taking one careful step after another, his heart thudding.

"Tolly, where are you?" he called out, listening, and then he thought he heard something.

"Down here!"

He was going in blind, and he knew Billy Jo would never forgive him if he didn't make it home. He shut his eyes and said a silent prayer. "I'm coming down! You have a gun?"

He thought he heard a laugh. "Wouldn't shoot you, Mark."

He took a step onto the ladder and climbed down.

Tolly was sitting on a stool, holding a gun, surrounded by piles of binders, files—and explosives.

"Just what do you think you're doing?" Mark said.

It wasn't bright, but the darkness couldn't hide the heaviness in Tolly's eyes as he said, "Told you. Cleaning up."

Mark fisted his hand at his side. He wanted to reach for his gun, but Tolly shook his head and lifted his own gun to his head.

"You're not faster than me, Mark," he said.

Mark pulled his gun from his holster and pointed it at Tolly. What the hell was going on? "How deep are you in this?" he said, his voice unusually calm.

Tolly shook his head, his gun pressed to his temple. "Deep enough that I'd hang. I know that much. You can't fix this, Mark."

Mark's finger was pressed to the side of the gun, ready to fire if needed, though he hoped he wouldn't. "You don't know that. Put the gun down. You have kids. What about Gail?"

Tolly shook his head, and a tear slid down his face. "She don't know nothing about this. I'm going to hell, Mark, one way or the other. This way, it's my choice."

"No, you're being a fucking coward. Why Elisha? Who sent her, you?" he said, not pulling his gaze from the gun Tolly had to his head. His finger was on the trigger, and he could see explosives beside him. A timer or a switch?

"No, I didn't know anything about her," Tolly said. "Never knew who all the players were. Mary Jane. Herb Walker. Tidus Huntley, Mary Jane's father, whose grandfather was the head of the council on this island—one of the forefathers, he bragged. Laura Fieldcrest, the heiress of the Cranston liquor dynasty, who owns the seventy-acre private estate on the west side, with the private dock and helicopter landing pad. Winston Kirsch, the federal judge. Dirk Engel, one of the Silicon Valley tycoons. Stuart Moral, head of the World Banking Group."

Mark knew he was frowning as he stared at the gun. An icy chill coursed through him at those names, the names of people who could make him and his family disappear permanently. "Tolly, look, I'm going to put my gun down, and then I need you to, as well. Let's just talk and sort this out." He flicked his safety back on and held his gun up in one hand, the other in the air. "Come on, Tolly. I can't talk if you're going to keep a gun to your head. Put it down, please."

He didn't think he would, but he did. He pulled his gun away and let it dangle at his side, and he held up his other hand, in which he was holding a dead man's switch.

"Tolly, are you planning on blowing us both up, all of this?"

The old chief looked over to Mark. For a big man, he suddenly looked so small. "You think I want to do this? I have kids. My daughter is pregnant and is expecting in the spring. I was looking forward to meeting my grandchild. No, I don't want this, but when they have something on you, they own you. These sick fucking bastards. This has been going on for generations, hundreds of years. This is bigger than you and me."

The cupboards were empty, and the doors behind the chief were open, leading to the cells where the kids had been kept. Mark knew he'd never get it out of his mind.

"How many kids, Tolly? They've been moving kids on and off this island. How does it work? Did you know Dr. Kolter was part of this? I found the toddler he bought, Pat…"

The chief let out a rough laugh before spitting out, "Kolter was part of fuck all. He was a fucking parasite they kept around because he did what they told him— checked the kids, kept them breathing for all those sick motherfuckers out there who prey on their innocence. There's a lot of evil out there, Mark, and they don't walk in the shadows. They make the laws you and I have to obey. You want to help that little girl you found, that little boy? You keep them out of the clutches of CPS."

Mark took in the explosives, the C4. It looked as if it had been set up by a professional, and he didn't think Tolly had any explosives experience. "You still didn't tell me how many kids you helped move. How long did the kids stay down here? How many, and where did they come from? And why is CPS sending a copy of all its reports to a private company via that fax machine right over there, the Hanover Foundation?"

Tolly pointed to the counter. "You ever ask yourself why an organization like child protective services was created? Sure, in the beginning, before the First World War, it started with rescuing a beaten and abused eight-year-old girl. In the 1930s, the federal government first ventured into child welfare, passing different laws and acts over the years, putting more money into agencies, funding a foster system in which kids could be picked off and no one would be looking for them. It's a huge front for an evil trafficking ring around the world.

"Some are raised in it as babies, born into it. Families sell their kids into it. Thousands, Mark, even millions around the world. You have no idea what happens here, how many kids are quietly moved and sold and shipped off in containers to fill an order for the super wealthy. It's a world you don't want to understand. At the ports, the shipping containers are marked *live art* so they can't be searched. Look into who passed that law. Do your homework.

"It's not just about taking the innocence of a child. You know this. It's about the illegal adoption of babies, about organ harvesting, about pure evil, the kinds of things that come from your worst nightmare. I never touched one child. I never moved one child. But you have any idea how many churches are only a front? Kyle moved anywhere from five to ten thousand kids a year through here, maybe more.

"The senate committee passed a bill giving funds to the private company that gets a copy of every report from child protective services. It's funded by the public. What better way to find a child to fill an order? Not many people question why a private company has been given access to children, because no one questions anything anymore. When I walked that social worker off this island, that sick fuck, I told myself I'd saved a few hundred kids. I knew I wasn't stopping it, but I thought I could play both sides.

"But it doesn't work that way, Mark. Don't call the Feds. You don't know who you can trust over there. The three-letter agencies don't work for who you think. That girl you caught, Trix, she wouldn't have felt an ounce of remorse for stabbing Kyle so many times. I looked. That was anger and vengeance. She had every right, but I don't think you can save her anymore after what has been done to her."

Mark kept his eye on the chief's left hand, on the switch. "What about Ollie McCormick, dead in the church? Funny thing, she had a kill list of my family in her hand. Trix said she wrote the list and put it there. She said she killed her, strangled her. But why did she think I was involved?"

The chief was looking right at him again. "She knew the chief was involved. She meant me. She had the wrong chief, but I'm sure you've figured that out. Trix, I don't know how many times she was sold. Ollie was who moved the kids. She befriended them—girls, mostly. All the kids knew her. She had that nurturing quality of a psychopath. In killing her, Trix did this world a favor, but there will be someone tomorrow to take her place.

"Mark, when your eyes are open, you see things in this world that aren't what you believed. One morning, you wonder if everything you've ever learned was a lie. Not all orphanages are just that. Those big international talent shows where parents send their kids, seeking fame and fortune…?" He shook his head. "You have to have both eyes open in this world."

He still didn't understand how Tolly Shephard could have looked away. "What did they have on you?"

"I left you something, Mark." He nodded to the fax machine.

Mark didn't want to look away, but he did, seeing a small thumb drive. He stepped over to the counter and reached for it, then held it up. "What is this?"

The chief held up his hand with the switch, and Mark felt his heart thud long and loud. He reminded himself to breathe and lifted his gun again.

"As soon as I let go of this, it blows," Tolly said. "This, down here, will never be used again. That thumb drive has evidence on everyone, all the names, all the countries involved, the kind of people you'd never believe could possibly be part of something like this. Most are untouchable. You have a choice. You can put it down and walk away, and you can return to that blissful, peaceful ignorance and pretend this isn't happening, or you can take it and never have a peaceful night's sleep again. You'll look over your shoulder, because if they know you know, you'll never see who's going to come after you or your family. The choice is yours, Mark. I didn't walk away, and they took one of my kids. They got me and my silence in exchange for my getting him back."

"Is Carmen involved? Trix told Billy Jo she heard her name."

Tolly shook his head. "No, but they know she suspects something. I assured them I'd keep her looking elsewhere. Gail will grieve. Be kind to her. Call the state troopers, and reach out to the sheriff's group I put you in touch with. The Feds will bury and spin this. McCormick and Drake will be said to be victims of crime, and Kolter might be touted as a hero. If you shoot me and this goes off, I'll end up taking you with me. But I like you, Mark, so go. I'll count to ten."

He shook his head. "No. We'll figure out another way…"

"One…" Tolly started.

Mark knew he'd never convince him. He holstered his gun and shoved the flash drive in his pocket, then reached for the ladder and climbed it.

"Two…."

He was on his knees in the dining room, seeing the table he'd moved the night before. He rolled to his feet.

"Three…"

He ran to the door, vaguely hearing the old chief still counting. He hit the door, and it flew open, and he stumbled out into the snow and kept going, running toward his Jeep. The snow was deep and hard to run through.

He didn't hear anything, but he felt the blast. The force threw him in the snow. It took him a second to roll over and see the flames, the smoke and the debris. His Jeep had pieces of wood on it, and the windshield was cracked. Mark sat up, taking in the destroyed house, and felt an emptiness he'd never felt before.

He reached into his pocket and pulled out his phone, then stood up and walked the rest of the way to his vehicle. He hovered over Carmen's number, but he only wanted to talk to one person.

He listened to the ring, then the groggy "Where are you?"

Damn, she always made him feel so good.

"I'm coming home. Just wanted to hear your voice," he said. He thought he heard her sit up. Maybe she was in bed.

"You okay? What happened?"

"Have I ever told you how much I love you?"

There was silence for a second. "You don't sound okay. You talked to Tolly?"

He shook his head as hollowness filled the center of his being for a man he'd never really had a fondness for. But he'd sacrificed himself, taking a secret to the grave with him. "Yeah, I talked to him. Look, I don't want to wait to get married. Let's find someone and just do this."

There was silence again. Then, "You sure?"

The wedding had always been for him, not her. "Yeah, I just want to marry you."

"Okay. I love you, Mark. See you soon."

As she hung up, Mark took in the smoldering debris. He walked around his Jeep, pulling off the pieces of shingle and wood from the house, and he climbed behind the wheel and started the engine. He stared down at his phone. Then he dialed the fire department.

"Yeah, this is Chief Friessen. I'm at the home of Kyle Drake, the minister. I need you to send a truck over. There's been an explosion," he said. Then he hung up, tossed his phone on the seat, put his Jeep in gear, and turned around.

## Epilogue

She stared in the full-length mirror at her image in the long white dress. It wasn't fancy. It was simple, but for the first time in her life, she felt beautiful, not the rough and tough Billy Jo. Her brown hair was loose with sprigs of baby's breath, and in the sandals on her feet, she could walk a step or two.

The door opened, and there were her mom and dad. They always had looked so good together.

"Wow, you are stunning," Chase said. "Mark is going to fall over when he sees you." He wore a navy suit, and her mom wore a silky pink sleeveless dress.

Rose was already starting to tan from the Mexican sun. She walked over to her and stood behind her, looking in the mirror at her.

"This is for you two and Mark's family," Billy Jo said. "We were all set to find a judge and just get it done, but no, you had to interfere and make some calls and book all this." She tried to sound mad, but she couldn't, because the resort was beautiful, and being away from

Roche Harbor right now was a gift after what they'd been through.

"I'll have you know this resort is all Jed and Diana," Chase said. "Apparently, it's a Friessen family venture. And sorry you didn't get to see a judge, call us to say you were married, and then get right back to work as if you'd just made a trip to the store."

Her mom rested both her hands on her shoulders.

Billy Jo wondered whether her dad was trying to make a point. "Now was not the time for us to leave, Dad…"

"Which is why I took your phone," Chase said, cutting her off. "You will never stop working."

It was true. She'd been texting and emailing nonstop to Lisa, Grant, and Pam, trying to work a miracle for Nathan and Grace. "Kids are important."

"Yes, they are, but so are you and Mark. There will always be more kids. And I shouldn't say this, but Pam sent you a text. Nathan and Grace are picking up both their kids. She said Grant made a call."

"You read my texts?" She turned around.

Her dad appeared suddenly exasperated. "Would you rather I ignored it and had you wondering all through the ceremony how you could sneak away and make a call? Because I knew you would."

She worked her mouth, fighting the urge to smile. Her dad knew her too well. "Thank you," she said.

Her mom kissed her cheek. "Okay, see you down at the beachfront," she said, then headed out of the bedroom of the penthouse suite of the top floor of the resort, leaving Billy Jo with her dad.

She walked over to the floor-to-ceiling window, seeing the man she loved down on the beach in front of an arch of flowers, his family around him. He was laughing with his brothers, and she spotted Pat's blond mop of hair. The girl was in J.D.'s arms, and Chris lifted up Jay to sit on his shoulders.

"You and Mark have a lifetime to right the wrongs in this world," Chase said, resting his hands on her shoulders.

She had to remind herself it was okay for her and Mark to leave even though Tolly Shephard had killed himself. Gail's grief had been horrible.

She didn't turn around. "Dad, there are so many people who are not going to want Elisha to talk. I know Mark gave you that flash drive. What are you going to do? I know Mark will turn over every rock to get that sick, evil shit off the island." She lifted her hand to the glass, then turned to look at her dad, whose gaze was serious.

"And he will," he said. "The state troopers have already arrested most of the council and a few more of the names Mark had. But this is bigger than Mark. The military will oversee it, not the Feds. Mark's role in this, and yours, is done. Trix, that poor girl, will hopefully get the help she needs. And you should know something. Chris and J.D. said they're adopting Jay and Pat."

Billy Jo dragged her gaze back to the window. She'd never forget how protective Chris had been when they'd walked through the door with the little girl.

"I would have talked Mark into keeping them," she said. "I didn't expect his brother to do it."

Danny, her dad, and Diana, all the lawyers in the family, seemed to know how to pull strings and move mountains.

"There will always be more kids who need you and

Mark," Chase said. "You will both do what you can. Some you can save, some you can't."

She turned away from the window and looked up to Chase. "I really love him, Dad."

He pulled her close and hugged her. "I know you do," he said, then stepped back and held his arm out. "Shall we go, or do you want to keep Mark waiting some more?"

She walked over to the side table, where a small bouquet of white and pink roses sat, and she picked them up and looked over to her dad, who was smiling at her. "No. I've kept him waiting long enough," she said, and she took his arm and walked out of the room, to the new beginning of team Billy Jo and Mark.

Turn the page for a sneak peek of
*THE CHARITY* the next book in the *BILLY JO MCCABE
MYSTERY*
*Available in print, eBook & audio*

keeps a watchful eye on all the residents and who comes and goes on his island. But when a stranger buys a large property on the west side of the island, Police Chief Mark Friessen shows up on his doorstep to find out the reasons he moved to the island.

Only Walter Crandall wants to keep a low profile, and to be left alone. He has a five year old daughter and an ex-wife on the island who owns the local bar. He says he's made mistakes and wants a chance to make amends. Only there is something about the man that Mark doesn't trust. But when Mark and Billy Jo begin digging into this man's past and the Charity he was part of, what they uncover is a deception that is so twisted both Mark and Billy Jo are convinced it couldn't possibly be true.

S leeping in was something Billy Jo didn't do, but for the past four days, Mark had opened his eyes to find his wife sound asleep. As he stood in the kitchen, the stove blinking a digital blue 8:10 a.m., he realized he needed to wake her soon.

The coffeemaker beeped, and Mark poured himself a cup of the steaming brew before turning back to the island, on which a file lay open, revealing notes on another thirty of the island's residents. Hesitating only a second, he wondered when he'd become that cop who went digging into civilians' lives, looking for any secrets they might have.

*Oh, yeah. When a bunch of criminal elites took up using his island as their personal playground.*

He had to roll his shoulders, feeling that punch in the gut again, silently hating the world of people who, at times, were untouchable.

"You didn't wake me."

He turned to see Billy Jo in a blue robe, yawning as

she walked sock-footed past him and pulled a glass from the cupboard to fill with water.

"Figured you needed sleep," he said. "Was going to give you another ten minutes before waking you. You feeling okay?"

She brushed her shoulder-length brown bed hair away from her face and shook her head before drinking down the water. "Fine. Just tossed and turned because of your snoring. What are you doing?"

She settled her glass in the sink, then reached for his coffee and took a swallow of it. As she looked down at the open file, her brow furrowed. He realized she wasn't giving the coffee back, and he couldn't believe she had tossed out that comment about his snoring, considering she had fallen asleep before him.

He leaned down and pressed a kiss to the top of her head, then filled a second mug, a matching green one, from the many wedding gifts that seemed to still be arriving daily from people on the island he'd met only a time or two.

"Looking into the folks who live here," he said, "why they live here, what they do, especially the ones who look too clean. Who lives here full time, part time, and what hidden secrets do they have? You know, the usual investigative thing I do, looking for red flags and skeletons."

Mark filled the mug with coffee and settled the carafe back on the burner. Billy Jo angled her head, glancing over to him in that way of hers. She was complex, with many moods, and he figured something else was coming.

"You were serious, then?" she said, flattening her hand over the file, the notes he'd been reading on

Shirley and Tom Campbell, and pulling it closer to her. "You're really going to investigate every person who lives here and dissect their lives even though they've done nothing wrong? Isn't there some law against that, let alone the fact that you're overstepping a bit?"

She didn't smile and didn't pull that fiery gaze from him. She was the complete package, a woman who was his best friend, his lover, his wife, and she knew how to push every one of his buttons. Damn, he loved everything about her.

He reached for the file in front of her and pulled it away. "Knowing who's on this island and what they're about is something I should have done long ago. You forget what happened here? I don't want that kind of evil ever sneaking in. So yeah, I plan to dissect the lives of everyone who lives here to make sure the members of this community are decent, honest, not looking to set up some criminal enterprise, thinking they can do anything. And that includes our politicians. Consider it my new pastime. I plan to find out everything about them, what they do, who they see, to really dig into their lives. If they are honest people, then they become the people I'm protecting. But how many more criminals are still here, so deep underground that I haven't found them yet? And *yet* is the key word."

She looked up at him, and a smile touched her lips as she leaned against the island, so close to him. "You know all the right things to say sometimes," she said. "Go dig and dissect the lives of anyone and everyone. Oh, and make sure, will you, that you take a second and third look at everyone collecting a check from the DCFS, and especially who rubber-stamped their approvals?"

"They're first on the list—kids and animals." He leaned down and kissed her forehead.

"You're the best," she said. "Damn, I'm going to be late." She lifted the mug and took a swallow. "Oh, and I forgot to tell you we're going to drop in and see Gail tonight. I'll swing by the station after I'm done and we'll head over. I told her we'll bring dinner…"

She had trailed off as she walked back to the bedroom. Then she turned in the doorway, looking back, when he hadn't said anything. The tightness that came every time he thought of Tolly Shephard returned deep in his chest. He knew he'd made a face.

"You have to figure out a way to get past that, Mark," she said. "Gail is our friend."

"Her husband was part of a child trafficking ring."

She let out a heavy sigh. "I know what Tolly Shephard did and didn't do—and what they did to his son to gain his compliance when he played both sides. He's dead, but Gail isn't, and she still has to get up every morning and come to terms with all the secrets Tolly had. Mark, you've turned this island upside down and woken up a lot of people to what has been happening behind their backs. No one saw it. The town council is in a state of flux. You have interim appointees, as the mayor and councilors are now charged, awaiting trial. The entire CPS department has been turned upside down, and jobs are still being vacated. You're a hero for the children, Mark, but you have to know many of the island folks have turned on Gail. Their anger is misdirected. Her truck was spray painted with *CHILD KILLER*. People she's known forever on the island have phoned and said some horrible things…"

"Someone vandalized her truck?" he cut in. "Why didn't she call me? When did this happen?"

Billy Jo glanced over to the window. Her three-legged cat was curled up on the cat tree, whereas Lucky had padded into the kitchen and was lapping water out of his dog bowl. She started back toward him in the fuzzy robe that was more warm than flattering, and he didn't know what to make of the shadow in her face. He knew well the places her head went when she struggled. What she was thinking, he had no idea.

"Gail won't phone you," she said. "Not that she thinks you wouldn't show up and file a report, because she knows you would, but I think she believes that because of what Tolly did, she deserves every hateful thing coming at her. Yet every time someone lashes out at her, it kills a little piece of her soul. I can see it. I know Tolly wasn't strong enough to end things the way you did. But I also know he hid it well. So tonight we'll take a pizza over, talk to her and be civilized, and let her know she's a human being and we care."

Maybe it was the way she'd said it, but he wondered whether she understood how he felt about Gail. He couldn't look at her without seeing Tolly.

Instead of saying something, he took another swallow of coffee.

"She thinks you hate her, Mark," Billy Jo said, striding back over to him. She put her mug down on the island, not looking away from what he knew was likely shock staring back at her.

"Excuse me?" he said. "I don't hate her. Where would she ever get an idea like that?"

Billy Jo took another step toward him, sliding her

hand on the island to touch the file again, likely seeing the names listed. "Maybe it's because you make excuses never to go and see her. I show up alone, and every time I do, she asks about you, and I feel like I'm cheating when I say you're great but busy, or else you'd be there too. She doesn't believe one word of it, because she can see in my face that I'm lying. Or maybe it's because the last time she saw you was when you told her about Tolly."

Mark pulled his hand over his face, knowing she was right. He could feel the heavy sigh of frustration before it passed his lips.

"You going to make me go alone?" Billy Jo said, pulling her arms over her chest, not looking away.

"I don't hate her," he said. "I just don't know what to say to her. There's a difference."

Billy Jo glanced away, pulling in a deep breath. Then she lifted her gaze, which had softened just a bit. "Sometimes just being there is all that's needed. Don't say anything. Don't pretend. Just pick up a piece of pizza and eat. Can you do that?"

He'd never known Billy Jo to be so reasonable. "I can do that."

She ran her hand over his arm, rose up on her tiptoes, and kissed his cheek. "Good. And you may also want to consider asking Gail to help you dig into the people here. Pick her brain," she said as she reached for her mug and topped it with more coffee.

He wondered if she'd lost her mind. "Breaking bread with Gail is one thing, Billy Jo, but I'm not having her anywhere near this." He knew it had come out rather sharply. He had felt the bite in his words.

Billy Jo blew on the steaming coffee and took a swallow. "Well, that's too bad, because I'm sure she could fill in a lot of holes about a lot of people that you wouldn't otherwise know. And it may help her feel as if she's doing something to make up for what Tolly did. It's a helpless feeling, Mark, feeling responsible even though it's not logical. You could dig and miss something Gail knows that you would never have figured out in a million years. She's been here, like, forever." She tapped his arm again. "Think about it, Mark. That's all I ask."

Then she walked away, and he watched her, her heavy socks, her warm housecoat. This time, she didn't look back.

He reached for the file, seeing the names, as the shower popped on.

"Yeah, there's no way I'm asking Tolly Shephard's widow for help when it comes to anyone on this island," he muttered. Lucky brushed his leg, then looked up at him and whined. "Now, don't go looking at me like that. We'll go see her, eat pizza, and then leave."

There it was again, that sinking feeling he got every time he thought of Gail. As he took in the open file and the notes that only scratched the surface, he couldn't help thinking Billy Jo was too often right. But he wouldn't ask Gail even though she could clear up a lot of questions about a lot of people.

No, involving Gail was exactly what he wasn't going to do.

# About the Author

"Lorhainne Eckhart is one of my go to authors when I want a guaranteed good book. So many twists and turns, but also so much love and such a strong sense of family."

(Lora W., Reviewer)

New York Times & USA Today bestseller Lorhainne Eckhart is best known for writing Raw Relatable Real Romance where "Morals and family are running themes." As one fan calls her, she is the "Queen of the family saga." (aherman) writing "the ups and downs of what goes on within a family but also with some suspense, angst and of course a bit of romance thrown in for good measure." Follow Lorhainne on Bookbub to receive alerts on New Releases and Sales and join her mailing list at LorhainneEckhart.com for her Monday Blog, all book news, giveaways and FREE reads. With over 120 books, audiobooks, and multiple series published and available at all, retailers now translated into six languages. She is a multiple recipient of the Readers' Favorite Award for Suspense and Romance, and lives in the Pacific Northwest on an island, is the mother of three, her oldest has autism and she is an advocate for never giving up on your dreams.

"Lorhainne Eckhart has this uncanny way of just hitting the spot every time with her books."

(Caroline L., Reviewer)

**The O'Connells:** *The O'Connells of Livingston, Montana are not your typical family. A riveting collection of stories surrounding the ups and downs of what goes on within a family but also with some suspense, angst and of course a bit of romance thrown in for good measure. "I thought I loved the Friessens, but I absolutely adore the O'Connell's. Each and every book has different genres of stories, but the one thing in common is how she is able to wrap it around the family, which is the heart of each story." (C. Logue)*

**The Friessens:** *An emotional big family*

romance series, the Friessen family siblings find their relationships tested, lay their hearts on the line, and discover lasting love! "Lorhainne Eckhart is one of my go to authors when I want a guaranteed good book. So many twists and turns, but also so much love and such a strong sense of family." (Lora W., Reviewer)

**The Parker Sisters:** The Parker Sisters are a close-knit family, and like any other family they have their ups and downs. Eckhart has crafted another intense family drama… "The character development is outstanding, and the emotional investment is high…" (Aherman, Reviewer)

**The McCabe Brothers:** Join the five McCabe siblings on their journeys to the dark and dangerous side of love! An intense, exhilarating collection of romantic thrillers you won't want to miss. — "Eckhart has a new series that is definitely worth the read. The queen of the family saga started this series with a spin-off of her wildly successful Friessen series." From a Readers' Favorite award—winning author and "queen of the family saga" (Aherman)

Lorhainne loves to hear from her readers! You can connect with me at:
www.LorhainneEckhart.com
lorhainneeckhart.le@gmail.com

Also by Lorhainne Eckhart

**The Outsider Series**
The Forgotten Child (Brad and Emily)
A Baby and a Wedding *(An Outsider Series Short)*
Fallen Hero (Andy, Jed, and Diana)
The Search *(An Outsider Series Short)*
The Awakening (Andy and Laura)
Secrets (Jed and Diana)
Runaway (Andy and Laura)
Overdue *(An Outsider Series Short)*
The Unexpected Storm (Neil and Candy)
The Wedding (Neil and Candy)

**The Friessens: A New Beginning**
The Deadline (Andy and Laura)
The Price to Love (Neil and Candy)
A Different Kind of Love (Brad and Emily)
A Vow of Love, A Friessen Family Christmas

**The Friessens**
The Reunion
The Bloodline (Andy & Laura)
The Promise (Diana & Jed)
The Business Plan (Neil & Candy)
The Decision (Brad & Emily)
First Love (Katy)
Family First
Leave the Light On
In the Moment

In the Family
In the Silence
In the Charm
Unexpected Consequences
It Was Always You
The First Time I Saw You
Welcome to My Arms
Welcome to Boston
I'll Always Love You
Ground Rules
A Reason to Breathe
You Are My Everything
Anything For You
The Homecoming
Stay Away From My Daughter
The Bad Boy
A Place of Our Own
The Visitor
All About Devon
Long Past Dawn
How to Heal a Heart
Keep Me In Your Heart

**The O'Connells**
The Neighbor
The Third Call
The Secret Husband
The Quiet Day
The Commitment
The Missing Father
The Hometown Hero
Justice
The Family Secret

The Fallen O'Connell
The Return of the O'Connells
And The She Was Gone
The Stalker
The O'Connell Family Christmas
The Girl Next Door
Broken Promises
The Gatekeeper

**The McCabe Brothers**
Don't Stop Me (Vic)
Don't Catch Me (Chase)
Don't Run From Me (Aaron)
Don't Hide From Me (Luc)
Don't Leave Me (Claudia)
Out of Time

**A Billy Jo McCabe Mystery**
Nothing As it Seems
Hiding in Plain Sight
The Cold Case
The Trap
Above the Law
The Stranger at the Door
The Children
The Last Stand
The Charity

**The Wilde Brothers**
The One (Joe and Margaret)
The Honeymoon, A Wilde Brothers Short
Friendly Fire (Logan and Julia)
Not Quite Married, A Wilde Brothers Short

A Matter of Trust (Ben and Carrie)
The Reckoning, A Wilde Brothers Christmas
Traded (Jake)
Unforgiven (Samuel)
The Holiday Bride

**Married in Montana**
His Promise
Love's Promise
A Promise of Forever

**The Parker Sisters**
Thrill of the Chase
The Dating Game
Play Hard to Get
What We Can't Have
Go Your Own Way
A June Wedding

**Kate & Walker**
One Night
Edge of Night
Last Night

**Walk the Right Road Series**
The Choice
Lost and Found
Merkaba
Bounty
Blown Away: The Final Chapter

**The Saved Series**
Saved

Vanished
Captured

**Single Titles**
He Came Back
Loving Christine

**For my German Readers**
Die Außenseiter-Reihe
Der Vergessene Junge
Der Gefallene Held

**For my French Readers**
L'ENFANT OUBLIÉ

9 781990 590498